LIGHT ASCENDS

THE CONCLUSION TO
The Testimonial & Darkness Descends

IRA S. HUBBARD

One Printers Way
Altona, MB R0G 0B0
Canada

www.friesenpress.com

ISBN
978-1-03-911689-4 (Hardcover)
978-1-03-911688-7 (Paperback)
978-1-03-911690-0 (eBook)

1. FICTION, CHRISTIAN, FANTASY

Distributed to the trade by The Ingram Book Company

ACKNOWLEDGMENT:

As I reach the end of this eight year journey, there are several people I would like to thank. From the beginning, I was fortunate to have support from numerous people. One person who did not live to see the end of my journey was Daisie Redden. She and I worked together, and was the first person to read the original draft of my first book, The Testimonial. Daisie, who liked to read herself, enriched me with a lot of feedback. Her input and insight into the characters I was trying to develop influenced me to make major changes in both the characters and the story. She and I discussed the outline for my second book, Darkness Descends, and some of her ideas were incorporated into this story as well. I sent her a copy of the second book and she texted me within days, having finished it and offering her continued insight into what she liked and what she didn't. Sadly, Daisie passed away a short time after the release of this book, but I will always be grateful for her ideas and helping a very amateur author on his first effort. Her influence ripples throughout all three books. Next is my big sis, Faye (Loretta for everyone else) Ventro who took the time to read the first two books, while working full time and offered valuable insights into the process. I love you sis. The next person I want to acknowledge Bethany Wood. Beth and I work together and she was the only person to read all three books for me in the original drafts. Beth has a great eye for grammar and her constructive criticism was very valuable to me. She is very thorough and has great attention to detail. Throughout the three books, she pointed out things that worked, things that didn't and made beneficial suggestions that improved the quality of the story in many ways. I made a major change in the original plan for the story based on her feedback and her influence is obvious in all three stories. Beth, thank you so much for all your help and support. For my last book, Light Ascends, I want to give a special thank you to Irvin Steiding. Irvin is also someone I used to work with. He read the first two books and discussed each with me, offering his thoughts on the story. As a former pastor, he offered many thoughts on the plot and was intrigued by the outline for the final book. One piece I had not worked out, involved the location for the final dedication of the child. Irvin and I discussed this and he came back a few days later with a well thought out idea, supported by factual evidence (he took the time to print his research and gave it all to me) which I was very grateful for. Due to his efforts, I used this location in the book.

I want to thank my mother and father. My father, Steve Hubbard is a hard working man and a caring father. The older I get the more I appreciate that I inherited his work ethic, which has helped me to overcome many personal flaws and made everything in my career possible. My mother had the idea for the title of the final book. Growing up, my mother Eulah Hubbard always made me believe in myself. We had many hard times when I was a child, but despite all our problems and my personal struggles, mom always reminded me that I was fundamentally okay and she always reminded me that success or failure would ultimately be up to me. She always made me feel I could do anything and has never stopped believing in me. I love you both very much.

My wife Amanda is the person I want to take every journey in life with. Thank you for your continued support throughout the three books. I have so enjoyed the family we have built together, I love you.

I want to close with a message to my grandchildren Kylah, Carter and the many I am sure will be born in the years to come. While this is a very amateur work, it was hard, difficult and took many hours. In the end, I did it because it was something I thought I could do and didn't want to leave this box unchecked in my life. If I can leave you all with one message, it is to never give up on yourself and don't be afraid to fail. I have failed at so many things in my life, but failure should not be feared. So much of what I have learned in life is due to failure and it can be a great teacher if you take time to learn the lessons from it. I have also been fortunate to succeed in many things. If you don't try to do the things you love, you will eventually regret it. Don't let anyone ever keep you from pursuing your dreams and goals. Your life is yours and in the end, you will have no one to blame for your regrets but yourself. I love you all very much.

Shaun Hubbard 2021

PROLOGUE

The light was everywhere. It was eternal. To the angels, it was as it had always been. They had always lived in it, had known nothing else. One specific angel was standing near the great throne, looking up into an even greater brightness from above that shone on them all. Everyone's eyes were on him.

His beauty was indescribable. As light emanated from his entire body, he was both powerful and beautiful. He was the most beautiful of all the angels. His flowing hair framed his perfect face. His gaze was fixed on the amazing brightness radiating from above him.

The battle had been long and hard. He had tried his best, but he just couldn't win it, not here. He knew his time was up. He would have to leave here soon. Michael had seen to that. Now, it was about how many he could take with him. He paused from what he was saying and glanced back.

The angels were lined into two neat rows that went out of sight and seemed to go on forever into the invisible horizon of brightness. He didn't need to see them all. He knew exactly how many there were. All were standing erect. All were loyal, unquestioning...until he decided to lead them.

This is my moment, he reminded himself, and he wasn't going to waste any of the spotlight he had put on himself. He screamed into the great light that came from the throne, "I will lead these angels.

I am the greatest of all angels. I will build a kingdom above yours, and I *will* rule!"

No reply.

He turned, observed the endless rows of angels, and, in his commanding voice, said, "His time is over. I am destined to replace him and lead you!"

The angels stood at attention in perfect silence. None moved. Not even a single wing flinched, and none acknowledged his voice.

"The time has come for us to stand together!"

Again, no one moved.

Undeterred, he took several steps away from the throne and, again, exclaimed, "He is finished. You all see it. He is the past. I am the future. We are the future, not him!"

A voice boomed from behind him that shook everything and made them all tremble, "Go! All who would join him be banished from here forever!"

Lucifer took several steps away from the throne and screamed, "Who is with me?!"

For a moment, no one moved. Then, far down, from the left row of angels, one stepped forward. For a moment, he stood alone. Then, another slowly stepped forward, then another. Slowly, many stepped forward from both sides.

Lucifer stood patiently, until he was sure he had all he was going to get. He had hoped for half, but he could tell he had only about a third. He would, however, make it work. He strode confidently down the middle of the two rows of angels. As he passed, the ones that had stepped forward fell in step behind him. As he walked out of sight of the throne and into the darkness beyond, one of the angels walking behind him asked, "What is our plan? What will we do?"

Lucifer, without turning, smiled broadly and answered, "This battle will not come easy, and it will take time. But he is getting ready to create something. It will be his proudest creation. Not many know of it, but I do. We will start there. He is going to call it 'man.' I don't know everything about it, but I know he plans to give it free will, which means, over time, I will own them. Then, when we have turned his proudest creation against him, we will return to retake our home!"

As they walked into the shadow, the angels behind him, already starting to darken, screamed in unison, "Hail Lucifer! Hail to our god!"

Chapter One

ᴜᴜᴀꜱʜɪɴɢᴛᴏɴ, D.C.

All eyes were on the President. He looked awful. He was in a nice suit with a crisply starched and pressed shirt. Despite his clothing, it was easy to see he was worn and tired. He pulled his reading glasses from his face and tossed them on the table in front of him. He looked up at the people around the conference table and simply asked, "What else?"

There was silence for a moment. Then, Michael repeated, "What else? Mr. President, isn't that enough?" When there was no answer, Michael continued, "Mr. President, the election is just a few weeks away. Aren't you worried? I mean, the country is very divided. You are in a deadlock with your opponent. The country doesn't understand why we've made no mention of the Middle East, and if our press secretary has to say 'no comment' one more time, I think the entire press corps will walk out."

The President responded, "That may not be such a bad thing."

In truth, he wasn't worried about the election at all. It had already been guaranteed for him. That's what was keeping him up at night. The President looked around the room. Then, he said, "I know this has been difficult. The nation has to stay on course. We can't let ourselves be dragged into another foreign war. Wall Street is teetering, and the smallest thing we do could trigger a recession or worse. This is an internal matter and —"

"Internal?"

Suddenly, all eyes went to the back of the room. The interruption was from Dan, the secretary of defense. He continued, "Mr. President, forgive me, but the Muslims are flying planes made in China and launching bombs made in Russia. The rest of the world is looking to us for leadership, and right now, from their point of view, there is none. It is well-known who is backing the Muslims, and it is also well-known who is not backing Israel. No one!" Sensing he may have gone too far, he sat back in his chair.

The President glared at Dan for a moment, as an awkward silence settled over the room. The President was angry at the secretary's disagreement with his policy, but he grew even angrier as he found himself agreeing with him. Surprisingly, he looked around the room and asked, "Anything else?"

Everyone sat in silence.

Then, the President said, "Thank you."

He rose, and they rose with him. Then, he walked out the door. As he moved down the hall, he was flanked by Secret Service agents on both sides. He looked to the one on his right and asked, "Bays, where is she now?"

"In class, sir. We have eyes on her," was the reply.

The President darted into another room, and the agents looked at each other as Agent Bays said, "I've never seen anyone so paranoid over their daughter."

❧

Chapter Two

MEXICO

The chubby man ran down a dirty street, papers and trash covering the ground beneath him. His long, oily, graying hair was wet with sweat, and he could smell the alcohol seeping out his pores. He had been drinking for the last few days. He knew he was being chased, knew he was prey. He stopped momentarily and looked around. Then, he continued. The men behind him were closing in, but he still had a nice lead.

As he rounded a corner, he tripped on the uneven ground and fell. The wind was knocked out of him, but he quickly recovered and continued on.

These streets had been packed with people just a few hours earlier, but now, in the middle of the night, everyone was passed out in their beds. He moved into an opening with an old rock fountain in the center. It was surrounded by the stone and wooden balconies of the two-story buildings overlooking the area. He suddenly came to a stop at the fountain. As he did, he slowly turned. A smile appeared on his face.

As the men chasing him caught up, the leader motioned, and the men spread out around him in a semi-circle as the man in front strode confidently to within about a foot of him. The man was young, twenties, he guessed. He had brown hair, combed straight back, and piercing blue eyes. He was an imposing man with a six-foot frame. This was Joseph.

Like so many of his brothers and sisters, he was traveling the world, trying to catch as many of the Satanists as he could. Tonight, as on so many other nights, they had only found imps. The true Satanists rarely made appearances and seemed to be making themselves more and more reclusive, leaving their traditional work in the hands of their less capable associates, who were basically mercenaries that worked mostly for money or drugs.

Joseph was only twenty-six. Commanding a unit at that age was rare. He was from Great Britain and spoke with a strong English accent. He came from Christian parents, who were somewhat disappointed when their baby boy did not choose to take up the ministry, like his father and grandfather.

This imp had murdered a Catholic priest just hours before, and Joseph was angry they hadn't gotten to him in time. They had him now, and he was going to face judgment for his crimes. As Joseph approached, he said, "We know who you are! We know what you did!"

The imp looked unimpressed and replied, "Well, apparently, you don't know how to keep your men out of a trap!"

At that moment, spotlights came on all around them. Suddenly, the square was flooded with light. Men appeared all around them, and the clicks of guns could be heard in every direction. Joseph felt his heart race. It was another ambush. So many of them had been lured into a trap, and so many had been killed in the last few months. It all started with their elite squad, which had been wiped out by Cain two months ago. Now across the world, it seemed they were being targeted and hunted in almost every country. All their intelligence suggested this person had worked alone, but now Joseph could see he and his men had become their latest victims.

As Joseph looked around, he could see men in every direction. He tried to estimate. There were, at least, thirty. With only ten men, counting himself, he thought about the odds of any of his men living, especially since they were outnumbered three to one. One man, who appeared to be the leader, came forward with a gun. Joseph's men were ready, but only Joseph had pulled his gun, and none were willing to try it now, especially not with so many guns trained on them.

The chubby man laughed. Then, he said, "You should see the look on your face right now, man." Then, the chubby man walked to the man who appeared to be the leader of these imps with the gun and motioned for him to give it to him.

The bald man, clean-shaven, who was well-dressed in a collared shirt and slacks, hesitated.

Then, the chubby man said, "Hey. Look. I got them here, just like I said I would. I just want to put one into golden boy over there."

The bald man hesitated. Then, he slowly gave the gun to the chubby man and loudly said, "Once he fires, you kill the rest. Don't stop shooting till there are none moving."

Joseph realized this man was a Satanist soldier. They were always easy to spot in a group of imps. They were always polished and well-dressed, and they always spoke with a commanding arrogance.

The chubby man took the gun, turned, and walked toward Joseph. The chubby man pushed the barrel into Joseph's forehead and, without hesitation, pulled the trigger, but nothing happened.

Confused, he withdrew the gun and pushed it into Joseph's face a second time, this time into his left cheek, and pulled the trigger again, but the gun did not fire. There was a brief moment of hesitation.

Then, the chubby man burst into laughter as he said, "This gun is jammed. Give me another."

The bald leader, growing impatient, shook his head, then loudly yelled, "Open fire!"

In the still night, nothing moved. Nothing made a sound. Joseph wanted to act; instead, he looked around, trying to figure out what was going on. Suddenly, grunts and groans could be heard.

The bald man looked confused and screamed again, "Fire!"

An imp flew into the fountain from above, his body making a sickening thud in the shallow water. There was a moment of silence as both the bald man and Joseph looked in stunned disbelief at the site.

Joseph wasn't sure what was going on, but he raised his gun and began shooting. All the Christian soldiers pulled their guns and did the same. No one was shooting back at them. In just a few moments, all the imps were on the ground, and the bald man stood frozen in front of Joseph. He didn't move. Joseph walked up to him and, after seeing slight twitches and jerks, realized he couldn't move. It was as if he was frozen where he was standing.

As the Christian soldiers formed a circle around him, weapons at the ready, Joseph slowly put his gun away. He wasn't sure what was going on. He looked around, into the night. As he scanned the tops of the buildings, he saw a figure looking down at him.

In the night, he could only make out a silhouette, but for some reason, he knew this person was a friend. The silhouette nodded at him, and as he turned back, the bald Satanist fell to his knees.

Joseph stared for a moment but understood. He pulled a blade from behind his back. Then, he went and stood behind the man. He grabbed the man's forehead and pulled it back with his left hand. With his blade raised high in his right hand, he said, "You have this one moment to repent. You have this one moment to ask for forgiveness."

The Satanist confidently replied, "No. No redemption. I know where I am going, and I have prepared for it my entire life. But, know this, he has been delivered unto us, and your days are numbered. Soon, you will all be erased, and we will begin our dominion over the Earth and eternity."

Joseph, looking solemn, said, "As you wish." Then, with one quick motion of his blade, he sent the man to eternity. Afterward, Joseph looked back up, but the silhouette was gone.

Chapter Three

BEIJING, CHINA

The Chairman was concluding a meeting, which had gone well. A man stood, smiled, and bowed. As he left her office, she walked to the window and let herself take in the view of this amazing city.

Lately, everything had been going well. The Christians were on the run. They were in complete control of the American president, and their plans for Israel were in motion. Everything was going according to plan. Then, there was her biggest win — the child, their savior. He was only two months old, but the efforts of her soldiers had paid off. They now controlled his destiny, and now, after many years in the shadows, they were ready to step out onto the world's stage and make it in their image.

There was still much to be done, but she had never felt more confident. It had cost them their entire fortune, built over the last seventy-five years, but the recently formed Arab coalition was poised to destroy Israel and, more importantly, Jerusalem.

Once the child was anointed in their sacred ceremony, they would begin to build his empire on Jerusalem's ashes. By the time he was old enough to understand his importance, Christianity would be mostly a memory, an old, outdated way of thinking that would have died out a generation before him. It was a vast, bold plan, but it had to begin with the destruction of Israel and the Christians.

She smiled to herself for a moment. Not only would she destroy them both, but she believed she could destroy them simultaneously. Everything was going as Satan had told them it would. She would be at the forefront of a new age, the last age, which would usher in the end of Christianity forever.

Chapter Four

Ⱳᴀꜱʜɪɴɢᴛᴏɴ, D.C.

The President exploded out a door and down a hallway. Several aides and staff were trying to keep up. One young lady said, "Sir, you are slightly behind schedule. Your next meeting has been waiting for over a half-hour. The ambassador is starting to become impatient."

The President stopped, looked at another aide, and asked, "And what about the other meeting?"

The aide nodded as she said, "In your office now, sir."

The President nodded thoughtfully. Then, he looked at his entourage and said, "Tell the ambassador he will need to wait a little longer."

As the President hurried back to his office, his staff exchanged nervous glances. Another in the group asked, "Which one of us is going to tell the ambassador?"

The President jogged up the stairs. Then, he briskly walked down the hallway. As he entered the Oval Office, the man stood, but the President motioned for him to sit. As the President sat, he took in the man. The President knew he had a stellar professional record, but whom he really only knew personally from reputation.

CIA Director Mike Barnes was a small man, only 5'6", but anyone that spent more than ten minutes with him quickly noticed he could be an imposing man. His strongly set jaw and intense, deep-set hazel eyes, along with his intriguing personality and uncompromising integrity, made him a formidable presence, and he left a lasting impression. He had brown hair, which he always kept somewhat long. It hung just off his collar and was always perfectly combed to the right side. He always wore a nicely pressed suit and stood with a very straight posture, which was a result of his time spent in the marines.

As a staunch Christian, his conservative views were well-known to all that knew him. He came from a wealthy family. His father had made his money on Wall Street, but Mike had decided to pursue a different path. Ivy League-educated and well-spoken, he radiated confidence in any subject.

While the two men had been in many briefings together, it occurred to the President that he had never been in a room alone with the man.

Mike, sensing the President's hesitation to speak, asked, "What can I do for you, Mr. President?"

The President, after being quiet for a moment longer, spoke slowly, "I appreciate you coming on such short notice. I need to ask a favor."

Mike nodded thoughtfully. Then, he replied, "Of course, what can I do?"

The President cleared his throat. Then, he spoke in a low voice, almost as if he were afraid someone was listening, "I need you to investigate someone in Congress."

Mike's mouth dropped open, but before Mike could speak, the President continued, "Don't tell me you can't and don't tell me you haven't before because I know both are not true. I wouldn't be asking if it were not a serious matter of national security."

Mike stiffened. A look crossed his face the President couldn't quite read, and he replied, "Mr. President, forgive me, but this seems like a job for the FBI."

The President nodded in agreement. "Yes, but I don't trust the FBI director. I need you to do this. I feel I can trust you."

Mike replied, "Mr. President, with all due respect, you don't know me."

The President nodded. "True, but I know enough. I know you are a man of principle, and right now, you are the best I have."

Mike stared at the President for a moment. Then, he asked, "Who would we be investigating?"

"Young," the President replied.

Mike gave him a suspicious look.

The President continued, "This is not politics. I have good reason to believe he is plotting against our country. I have no proof of this, but I know it to be true. I need you to investigate and bring me proof. He is not alone. I need you to find his co-conspirators and help me bring them to justice."

Mike stared at him for a long moment. Then, he said, "Mr. President, what you are asking is very inappropriate, but because you are telling me this man is a threat to national security, I will make some discreet inquiries. I won't promise anything, but I will use our resources to find out if there is any credibility to these accusations. Forgive me, Mr. President, but I must also add, if I find any evidence this is personal or political, I will cease all inquiries immediately and report this request."

The President nodded thoughtfully as Mike finished speaking. Then, Mike moved to the door. As he reached the door, he turned and asked the President, "I still don't understand, Mr. President. Why me?"

The President stared at him for a moment and let out a sigh. Then, he replied, "Because you are a Christian."

Mike returned the stare for a moment. Then, he nodded, turned, and left the room.

Chapter Five

BRAZIL

David was sweating. He moved his hand to his forehead and wiped the perspiration away, but it kept coming. He was nervous. The elevator was old and screeched as it started and stopped on the various floors. It seemed to go on forever. He knew she was on the top floor. He had originally heard she was dead, but recently, he'd learned God had saved her again. She should have died more than once, but for some reason, God kept her alive. He heard she had suffered what were believed to be mortal injuries. The helicopter pilot that found her actually thought she was dead. He had given her only moments to live, and she had whispered some final words, but miraculously, she had lived. All that had happened a couple months ago.

She was in the hospital here. Her condition was too severe for her to be moved. He had wanted to see her, but he was wanted, wanted by both sides now. He had spent the last two months in prayer. He had worked to get closer to God. He needed to know his purpose. He needed to know what it was God needed from him, what his role was to be.

His power had never left him. He could access it easily. He still didn't fully understand it, but it was in every fiber of his being. He owed that to his father. The irony of it all was never lost on him. He thought about it every day. His father, a lifelong and loyal Satanist, had reawakened the power within him, which had never ceased. He felt closer to God than ever before, and the closeness continued to grow. God walked with him now, and David felt the same comfort many Christians felt in their daily walks. David knew God was with all his children. He was trying to talk to God, trying to get more answers. He still wasn't getting them all, but he now understood more and more about everything that was going on around him.

The elevator dinged, and it jolted him out of his thoughts. He stepped off the elevator cautiously and looked both ways. The dingy white walls and poor lighting actually made him feel a little safer, like he could not be seen as easily here. He looked down the hallway to his right and saw all the burnt-out florescent light bulbs and heard the hum of the remaining lights but nothing else. He knew coming in the middle of the night would be the safest time.

He quietly walked down the hallway. Then, he turned the corner and stopped in front of the room he knew she was in. He was nervous. He didn't know what to say to her. He didn't know what she would say to him. The last time he'd seen her, he couldn't have imagined this was where they would meet again.

He put his hand on the doorknob and tried to open it gently, slowly, quietly, but it creaked and groaned. In the utter silence of the hospital, David cringed, fearing the loud door would wake everyone on the floor. After he'd opened the door just enough to fit his body through, he stopped and slowly looked around. He didn't hear or see any movement, so he stepped inside.

There she was, lying on the bed. Her back was to him. Her black hair was fanned out on a pillow. David just stared at her for a minute. He hoped he was looking at a friend, but he didn't know. He slowly approached her and put a hand on her shoulder. She didn't move. He nudged her a little harder, and she turned over.

15

In the dimly lit room, he saw Ruth's face, and it overwhelmed him. He felt himself unconsciously stagger back until his back hit a wall with a thump. He had missed her so bad. He loved her so much. Then, he heard her voice, "David? David, is that you?" She reached for a pull chain that turned on a dim light over her head, and now they could see each other more clearly.

Her voice had snapped David out of his vision of Ruth. He felt his legs weaken, so he grabbed a small wooden chair that was nearby, placed it behind him, and sat down.

Incredulous, Eve asked, "David?! What are you doing here?"

For a moment, David just stared at her, just stared to see if he was really seeing Eve. He wanted her to be Ruth, but he knew she wasn't.

Momentarily stunned by his vision, he finally asked, "How are you feeling?"

Now she just stared at him. Half-asleep, half-awake, and uncertain of what to say, she replied, "I'm healing. I'm almost ready to leave."

"I'm surprised they haven't transferred you back to a hospital in Tel Aviv."

Eve continued with a suspicious stare. She was shocked by his visit and was unsure what to say to him. He had been watching her. She knew that for sure. The guards that had been posted had just been removed a few days ago. He had been watching and waiting for the right time to come here, to confront her, but for what?

Neither spoke for several awkward minutes.

Finally, Eve broke the silence and repeated, "David, what are you doing here? What is it you want?"

David replied quickly, "Answers. I need answers to what happened to Ruth, to what happened to you. I'm trying to figure out how she died."

Eve pondered the question. She wasn't sure what she could say. She wasn't sure what she should tell him. Finally, she sat up in the bed, cleared her throat, and asked, "What do you know?"

David said, "I know she died and that she was with you. I heard she fell off a train and that you were with her at the end. I tried to find you right after, but then, I heard you had been killed, too." After a pause, he continued, "Then, I heard that was wrong and you were still alive."

Eve listened, and for a moment, his questions made sense, as she processed it all. She had a moment of shock when it hit her. She thought, He doesn't know. How is that possible? While trying to hide her surprise, she looked at him. But, if he knew, wouldn't that be the first question? she wondered. She cleared her throat a second time, trying to buy herself a few moments. Her thoughts went to Ruth. She knew Ruth would want him to know, but was this the right time, the right place? She spoke softly, "She didn't fall. She jumped. At least, that's what I believe."

David looked at her incredulously, "Why?"

Eve was certain of her conclusion now and continued in a voice that was almost as soft as a whisper, "I think to get away from him, to keep…" She hesitated. "Herself safe. She must have felt cornered, felt there were no other options."

David dropped his head, processing it all. She waited for him to raise it again. It took longer than she expected, but when he finally raised it again, he asked, "What happened to you? Where's your team?"

Eve felt a tear roll down her cheek before she had time to reply. This was something that was always on her mind. She replied to his question in a hoarse voice, "Cain."

That one word was enough. David instantly understood. He repeated, "Cain."

A moment of silence settled between them.

After a few moments, David asked, "How many survived?"

Eve felt more tears now. She looked at him through tear-filled eyes and made no effort to wipe them away. Her voice cracked as she said, "Just me. I don't know why. I should have died with them."

David felt his body unconsciously twitch. He felt anger, frustration, and confusion all at once. He was trying to process it all as he pondered the implications of all he had been told. He slid the chair over, closer to the bed, so he could put his hand on her. He touched her shoulder and said, "I know they would be glad you survived."

She looked at him incredulously. Then, she somberly said, "You didn't know them as well as I did. They were my responsibility, and I led them to their deaths. They trusted me, and I got them all killed."

David replied, "You know it isn't that simple, especially when Cain is involved."

She hadn't really discussed this with anyone, not really, not in-depth. Eve had held this in and wanted to say something to someone. Everyone kept telling her it wasn't her fault, but deep down, she couldn't accept that. She was their leader. Maybe another leader would have saved them, kept them safe, at least, some of them. She went back to that night. As the memories flooded her mind, she sobbed uncontrollably.

David instinctively pulled her to him and held her for a moment. While he tried to think of what to say, he just let her cry for a while. Then, as he sensed that she was calming down, he said, "I don't know about everything that happened, but I know they are in a better place and they are watching us now. I know they will want you to find a way to put this behind you and move on with your life."

She raised her head off his shoulder, which was wet with her tears. She asked, "What is my life now? What am I supposed to do? I had one job, to lead these men, these elite soldiers of God, and now they are all gone!" She started to sob again.

David didn't know what to say. He asked God to give him some words. Then, without thinking, he grabbed her face, which startled her. He looked in her eyes and firmly said, "They're not all gone. One is still here, still here because that is how God wanted it. You move on by remembering who we serve and why."

Eve's eyes widened. She seemed shocked by his statement.

In truth, David was shocked, too. He didn't know where that had come from.

Eve sat back into her bed and started rubbing her face. She was reflecting on everything that had happened in those last few days. She said, "We knew something was coming. We could all feel it. We thought we were going to fight the Satanist Elites. We didn't know it was Cain. Now, they have another advantage over us."

David took in a deep breath. After reflecting for a moment, he asked, "The soldiers in all white?"

As Eve nodded, David thought about it for a moment. Then, he said, "No. They don't have that advantage."

Eve looked at him, not knowing what to expect and feeling some suspicion. She asked, "How could you know that?"

David replied, "Because I was there when they died."

Eve stared at him hard.

Then, David murmured, "I killed them."

Eve's eyes widened. Then, as the shock faded, she asked, "All by yourself?"

As David nodded his head, Eve felt a chill go over her entire body, and she instinctively pulled her covers up around her stomach, as if trying to protect herself. Her head spun as she pictured David killing those men the way her men were killed. She should have felt some satisfaction at this, but for some reason, she didn't, and it scared her. She pondered the consequences. Was David Cain? Was Cain David? Could it be they were the same? She realized why the Christians feared him. She considered her own safety, but inexplicably, something about David made her feel safe. She had not felt threatened since he had walked through the door.

They both sat there, staring at each other, as if neither knew what they were supposed to talk about next.

David broke the silence and asked, "Why are they hunting me?"

The question was one she had been anticipating, but she didn't know how to reply. She cleared her throat again but felt he would see this as an obvious delaying tactic, so she answered quickly, "They found out about you and Ruth."

David had considered this to be one of the reasons but didn't understand why they would spend the kind of resources they had on one man. He asked, "How?"

Eve replied, "That's your response. 'How?' Does it matter?"

David looked somberly at her and replied, "It matters to me. Did Ruth tell you?"

Eve felt worry build within her. These questions were backing her into a corner, a corner that would leave her with no answer. She changed the subject and said, "David, you need to turn yourself in. You need to go to the Apostle and let him help you."

David replied, "Every soldier I have seen is heavily armed, and none look like helping me is what they intend."

Eve, feeling very tired now, bowed her head and said, "Much is at stake."

David seemed to accept this, at least, for now. He patted her arm and said, "Be well." He rose and started for the door.

Eve asked, "Where will you go now?"

David shook his head solemnly. He had no idea. Before opening the door, he tossed a small flip phone onto her bed. It landed at the base of the bed, at her feet.

She leaned forward, picked it up, and looked back up at him.

David said, "There is only one number in it. Call it if you need me but only if it is an emergency."

Eve nodded, not sure how to respond to this.

David moved to the door, and as he pushed it open, Eve said, "Her last thoughts were of you. She loved you."

David looked back at her, smiled, and nodded. Then, he walked out the room.

Chapter Six

TEL AVIV, ISRAEL

Joseph was giving his report to the Apostolate. Their mission had been a success, which had been a rarity lately, but the tone was still somber. Positive outcomes had mostly eluded them as of late, and he knew, while this was good news, there was a dark cloud that seemed to be hanging over them. Joseph looked around the room, cleared his throat, and said, "I have to emphasize none of this would have been possible without him."

The Apostolate exchanged glances with one another.

Then, Joseph continued, "They had us. They would have killed us if he had not intervened." His words were met with silence. Joseph nervously continued, "We have been hunting him, but he keeps helping us. Have we considered —"

"That will be all. The Apostolate appreciates your report," Job interrupted.

Joseph looked around for a moment. Then, he nodded and left the room. All eyes moved to the Apostle, who was in deep thought. He had been mostly silent during Joseph's report. After he sucked in a long breath of air, he looked around the room. Then, in a low tone, he said, "Few outside of this room know how bad it is for us now. Like Israel, we stand alone, outnumbered and outgunned. We face

22

an opponent with superior resources, who seems to be outmatching us regularly, despite this recent victory." He paused to see if there was a comment from anyone. When no one spoke up, he continued, "We have to acknowledge that David is not behaving like someone who has betrayed us. He took the initiative to help us, to save the life of our people."

Job, the most vocal member of the Apostolate, spoke up, "The walls are caving in all around us. We can't afford any mistakes. We can't just embrace him."

The Apostle responded, "I'm not asking for us to embrace him, but I am saying we need to hear his side of things. We need to know what he knows, what he has seen, and what his intentions are." He looked around the room. Then, he said, "I am going to pray about it, but I think we should bring him in."

Before anyone else could speak, he rose and left the room.

Chapter Seven

BEIJING, CHINA

The child rarely cried. He just seemed to eat, use his diaper, and sleep. Judas thought, This is how it must be with all children that are this young, as he stared at the child intently.

The woman caring for the baby was unnerved by Judas. He would do this often. This hideous, disfigured man would sit and stare at the helpless infant, but he never wanted to hold him.

Judas was in awe of the child. This child, his grandchild, was the long-awaited savior of his people, the child Lucifer had told them was destined to come. Judas knew the baby would be going on his first long trip soon. The time was coming to anoint the new king, and all knew there was only one place where that could happen. Judas thought of the world the child would grow up in, a world free of Christianity, Judaism, and, eventually, all other faiths. The time for their domination of the world was about to begin, and one day, this infant would oversee it all, a one-world government. This child would be the head, and Lucifer would be the god who ruled the world.

Judas smiled, as he thought about how his own sacrifices had not been in vain. He was thinking about his legacy now, and he could see the future in his grandchild, who was destined to rule the world.

The smile faded, and for reasons he could not explain, his thoughts drifted to the baby's grandmother. Judas looked into the boy's eyes. He looked like his father, and his father looked like her. Judas tried hard to block it out, but on occasion, he couldn't help but see a small part of her in this child. It was so ironic for him. He had worked very hard to put her out of his mind, out of his dreams. Judas drifted now and let himself think of her for a moment. He remembered her beauty, remembered his love for her. This was their grandchild, a descendant of the family they had made all those years ago.

When he allowed himself to go to that place in his mind, to go to her, he realized it was the only time in his life he had been truly happy. This child represented that happiness. Her face was in this infant's face, and every time he looked at him, he felt he was looking at her. This child represented everything they had made together. This child was the end result of their family, a family that was shattered now. As he thought of that, the way his oldest son had forced him to end his life and the way his youngest son had betrayed him, he came back to the hate, back to the reason for it all. No, he would not give in to weak-minded thoughts. He would finish what he had started, and this child would make up for the weaknesses of his grandmother, uncle, and father. This child would take his place, his rightful place, on the throne and oversee the entire world.

Chapter Eight

WASHINGTON, D.C.

The President was in the middle of a policy briefing when an aide entered the room, moved quietly across the room, and whispered in the President's ear, "I'm sorry, sir. Director Barnes is in your office and says he must speak with you immediately."

The President nodded. Then, he excused himself from the meeting. As he entered his office, Barnes rose, and the President moved swiftly across the room and asked, "What can I do for you, Mike?"

The director nervously replied, "Mr. President, I've begun looking into the person we discussed. I have, very quickly, hit a series of walls. He is well-protected, and I have been told discreetly that I should cease all inquiries."

The President felt his heart race. He was "poking the bear," and he sensed now was the time to either stop or push forward. He whistled softly. Then, he asked, "Mike, can you push forward and get past some of these obstacles?"

Mike nodded thoughtfully. "I think so, sir. I have a lot of resources, and I think I can try some other avenues to approach this investigation, but I felt you should know. I am sure he knows you are trying to look into him."

The President felt his heart race again as the possible retaliation he might face for his actions hit him. He placed a hand on Director Barnes's shoulder and said, "Proceed and do use all possible caution on the investigation and for yourself."

Chapter Nine

✝el Auiu, Israel

Eve was met at the airport by a small detail of soldiers, who would escort her back for her meeting with the Apostolate. As she stepped off the escalator, she saw the teenage-looking, fresh-faced young men waiting on her, looking around nervously and holding a small sign that simply read "Eve." She walked up and nodded.

As she and the three young men walked through the mostly empty terminal, Eve looked around, still reeling from her flight on the rickety private plane they had rented to get her home. To no one in particular, she said, "This place looks nearly deserted."

One of the young men responded, "There are no commercial flights coming into Tel Aviv International Airport. They have been cut off, due to the pending invasion."

Eve felt a chill run up her spine as she thought, So it is actually happening.

As she entered the compound on the other side of town, she was met by the Apostle, who gave her a warm handshake and a hug. He said,

"Eve, we are so happy to have you back. I certainly wish your return was under better circumstances."

Eve nodded solemnly and simply replied, "Yes."

Two hours later, her debrief was concluding with the murders of her men and her own injuries, all by Cain's hands.

One of the Apostolate said, "We were told you were found by a helicopter pilot on the tarmac."

Eve wiped tears from her eyes and nodded. Then, she said, "I couldn't speak, but I heard him pray a final prayer for me. I heard him tell the medics he knew I wouldn't make it because my wounds were too serious. I blacked out a few moments later and awoke in the hospital there."

Another member said, "Praise God," and this expression was repeated by all.

Eve was puzzled, as her eyes scanned the room, looking at each of them. Then, leveling her eyes at the Apostle, she asked, "Why?"

The Apostolate exchanged confused looks, and Eve asked again, "Why was I spared? I should have died with my men, the men I let die."

They all exchanged looks again, but no one spoke.

In truth, Eve was desperate to hear something. She wanted to feel like there was some reason God had kept her alive, but there didn't seem to be any she could find.

The Apostle finally spoke, "Eve, as you know, we don't always know God's master plan for us, but he will reveal it in time. You have to put your trust in him, and he will guide you."

Eve nodded but wanted more. The burden of losing her men was too much to bear, and she was close to crumbling in its wake.

The Apostle said, "So I think that covers everything."

Eve shook her head. "No, there is more. David came to see me." With surprised looks breaking out all around her, she continued, "In the hospital."

Job quickly asked, "What did he say?"

Eve began to cry again as she answered, "He wanted to know about my men, what happened to them. He wanted to know about Ruth. He had some limited information, but he was unclear on exactly what happened. He killed the Satanist Elite soldiers all by himself." Shock washed over everyone around her, and before another question could be asked, Eve blurted out, "He doesn't know."

Everyone on the Apostolate instantly understood as gasps and surprised looks broke out all around her. The Apostle leaned forward with an intense stare and asked, "How certain are you about this?"

Eve, still crying, wiped her eyes again and said, "I felt he was being honest. He has no idea about the child."

The Apostle continued to stare intently. Then, he slowly sat back and looked upward, thinking. The room broke out into debate as the meeting turned to chaos. Eve, looking around, noticed the Apostle was the only one not participating in the lively discussions.

After a few moments, he took the palm of his hand and hit the table hard. As silence settled and all eyes looked toward him, he said in a low, calm voice, "I want him brought here as soon as possible. Put the word out. We no longer view David as an enemy, but we do want him to come back here to meet with us."

Job said, "I must object to this. What if this is just a ploy for him to get inside these walls and kill us all?"

The Apostle coldly replied, "This is now a briefing. I am not asking for your counsel. I want him brought here as quickly as we can manage it."

The room, again, fell into silence.

Chapter Ten

BEIJING, CHINA

C ain strode confidently into the Chairman's office. She was not fond of him. They both knew this, but they did share a mutual respect that was rare for them both. He saw her as a good leader, and he believed Satan was working through her. She saw him as a great asset, a tool belonging to her master that she had to wield, at times, with great difficulty, to achieve their goals. Sometimes, she thought he was her ultimate trial to endure.

After Cain took a seat directly in front of her desk, he put one of his large boots up on her desk.

She took a deep breath and began, "Everything is going according to our plans. We have had to pour all our resources into this, but the payoff will be more than worth it. The Christians are stretched impossibly thin, and we have them spread out all over the world, in a vain attempt to engage us."

Cain nodded thoughtfully but didn't comment, so she continued, "The time is upon us. Our people will manipulate the Arabs into launching a joint attack on Tel Aviv and Jerusalem. Once the epicenter of Judaism, Islam, and Christianity is back in their hands, we will move to finish the Christians. Once they are out of the way, our people will easily secure the rest of the world, and our master can make his triumphant return."

Cain stared at her thoughtfully. This was not his normal demeanor with her, but the words carried tremendous weight, so she waited for him to speak. After a long silence, he dropped his large boot from the desk to the floor with a thud and asked, "What about David?"

The question surprised her. It was one she was not prepared for, so she deflected, "What about him? He is in the wind."

Cain replied, "He is the X-factor for them. He wiped out our best unit, and Judas's failure to kill him should have resulted in his own death."

She took that in for a moment. Then, she responded flatly, "If that were the case, we would have to kill you as well. You, also, failed to kill him, did you not?"

Cain glared at her, and she saw him grab the sides of his chair with white knuckles, fighting back the urge to lunge at her. She had to force herself to take another long, patient breath. No one looked at or talked to her like this, except Cain, and she hated it. Anytime she was alone with him, she had to remind herself this was her master's greatest test. Cain didn't know it, but he was her tool, her asset, provided for her to utilize in any way she saw fit, but he had always been difficult to handle, and his power, his enormous power, made him very arrogant. She let a thin smile pass her lips as she said, "All our intelligence suggests he is isolated and being hunted by the Christians. Right now, he is causing them to spread their already thin resources, even further, and if anything, he is helping us."

Cain leaned forward and said, "You can't think it is really that simple. Do you really think, Jehovah, Jesus, whomever you want to say is our ultimate enemy, is going to let all this go down with him on the sidelines?! You're incapable of that level of stupidity."

Her blood boiled, and instantly, she considered trying to have him killed. She had reached her limit. She was the most powerful woman on Earth, and she would command respect from him. He would treat her as the leader and powerful person she knew she was.

Unbeknownst to Cain, she had set up a button in her office for just this occasion. Not a button that would bring soldiers or some weapon, no, that would never work. This button that was under her desk, with one push, would summon a petite woman with drinks. These drinks would contain a poison that would kill Cain within sixty seconds.

She put her left hand gently under the desk and, with her middle finger, began to feel for the button. Her other fingers joined in, and she moved them around the button in a circular motion. One push and this would all be over. One push and she could stand over him as he gasped for his last breaths, knowing she had won in the end, and for the rest of her life, no one would ever speak to her this way again. The sensation was overwhelming for a short moment, and it made her feel pure bliss.

Then, as she pondered the long-term implications of his death, it passed, as it always did. She slowly relaxed back into her chair. She had passed another test. She silently thanked Satan for giving her the wisdom to continue. Now confident she had passed another test, she began to speak again, "Cain, the pieces are in place, and the final curtain will drop soon. With our help, the Muslims will finally destroy Israel. We have neutralized the U.S., and we will soon be going to anoint our master's earthly vessel. Even the Christian Bible understood we would have the child who will rule the world and make him into our master's image. In the coming days, we will witness all this come to pass. Whatever role David was going to play is played out. If he decides to reinsert himself into this, it will be too late. Indeed, it is already too late."

Cain looked at her for a moment. Then, he stood and walked to her door. Without looking back, he asked, "Anything else?"

Looking at him with some disgust and knowing he wasn't asking for permission, she said simply, "No, you can go."

As he turned the knob to walk out, Cain said, "I hope you are right about this because, if you are wrong, this whole thing could still blow up in our faces, and we all know how our master feels about failures." With that, he left the room.

Chapter Eleven

⊬ЄL ᴀUIU, ISRᴀЄL

Eve was in her simple, plain room. The last time she was here, which was only a couple months ago, the world felt very different. At that time, the world had not yet turned on their host country, David was with them, and her men were still alive. She thought about that for a moment as she walked to the water basin and splashed water on her face. When she heard a knock at her door, she quickly grabbed a towel, dried her face, and proceeded to answer it. When she opened the door, the Apostle was standing patiently on the other side, he asked, "May I come in?"

She quickly stepped aside and replied, "Of course."

He entered and immediately took in her room. He observed, "We left it just as you had it. No one came in here or touched any of your things, not even to clean."

She nodded. He motioned to a couple of wooden chairs in what passed for her kitchen. In truth, it was a water basin, a small, dorm-type refrigerator, and a few plastic plates and cups scattered on a tiny oval table. He asked, "May we sit?" She nodded again. As they sat, he began, "We don't have much time. I think the attack on Israel will be launched in a matter of days. All the signs are coming to pass, and we will have to make a last stand somewhere."

She nodded but didn't respond.

He continued, "I have been praying and seeking God's guidance more these last few days than I ever have in my entire life. I have come to believe he wants me to bring David in, maybe to help him. I don't know."

Eve just stared at the Apostle. She was beginning to understand where he was going, and now she anticipated the question he was about to ask: "Do you know how to get in contact with him?"

"Yes," she replied quickly. Then, she added, "But I won't bring him into a trap."

The Apostle nodded his head and agreed, "Neither will I. I wish we had more time, but the reality is we don't, and I think God still wants him to be involved and maybe help in all this. His powers are extraordinary, and even though he has sinned, he has also consistently rejected the Satanists. It's possible I may have judged him too harshly, but whatever he is going to do, we need to find out now, before it's too late. We may be able to help him find his way, and then maybe, he can help us."

Eve nodded her agreement. "I will try to reach him and ask if he will make contact with you."

Chapter Twelve

WASHINGTON, D.C.

The President was in his office, meeting with some aides, when his door burst open and Senator Morris Young entered, followed closely by the President's secretary, a mild-mannered woman who apologized, saying, "I'm sorry, sir. I told him you were busy, but he burst right in."

The President motioned for her to leave as he said, "It's okay. Morris, what do you want?"

Young nodded at the aides, and the President said, "Give us the room for a moment."

The aides quickly gathered some loose items and rushed out of the room. Young moved swiftly to the seat facing the President's desk and sat down. He began, "I thought you understood us, understood your place in things. I thought you understood how bad it would be to underestimate us."

The President looked at him, stone-faced.

Young continued, "You had Director Barnes looking into me, trying to find out what? Some piece of information you would use to blackmail me?"

The President continued his icy stare.

Young said, "Our patience for you is wearing thin. You will accept and execute this new role, and if you don't, there will be consequences."

The President didn't know how to respond, but inside, he felt encouraged. If Young was confronting him in this way, there must have been something he was worried he would find. He was moving in the right direction, and now, despite Young's desire to scare him, it was having the opposite effect. A thin smile appeared on the President's lips, and he finally spoke, "Maybe it is you who have underestimated me."

Young smiled broadly and replied, "No, it's not."

With this, he got up and grabbed a remote control that was lying on the President's desk. He looked at his watch, making a show of making a slight adjustment, and again, the President could see the Latin insignia that marked Young's people. He had seen it before and knew there were a lot of them in every part of the government.

Young sighed slightly as he said, "I think it's time."

He turned and activated the television that was mounted on a nearby wall. He flipped through a few channels until he found a news show. He tossed the remote onto the President's desk and said, "I told you once before that my name is Senator Young. This is your last warning. Call me 'Morris' again, and you will pay." The look in his eyes was cold and calculating. He adjusted his tie. Then, he left the room.

The President was confused. He grabbed the remote and turned up the volume. The reporter was talking about exploding gas prices, due to the impending conflict in the Middle East. The President, still puzzled, continued to watch as the news switched to a live report. The reporter began, "We are being told CIA Director Mike Barnes was killed in a car accident near Washington, D.C."

The President collapsed into his chair, as his head spun. He looked up at the ceiling as he pondered this and realized he had gotten Barnes killed. Then, the President turned and vomited all over the floor.

Chapter Thirteen

+€HRAN, IRAN

The man's name was Mohammad El Aziz. He was the general, the man designated to lead the assault on Israel. He was a short man. He stood only five feet, eight inches with black hair and surprisingly soft eyes.

As he looked at the wall full of monitors in front of him, his attention was focused on the largest monitor in the center of the room. It showed the greatest concentration of troops and known firepower surrounding Israel from all sides. Time was on their side, and he would not attack until everything was perfect.

As a top general in Iran's feared Elite Guard, he was selected for the top post from among a few other candidates. He relished the opportunity in front of him.

His father, a military man like himself, had not lived to see this. He had died just last year, but his mother was still alive. She had named him Mohammad, after the prophet. The great prophet, he thought.

It all went back to Abraham. Every school child knew that. He was the only person in both the Quran and the Bible. Both claimed he was the father of their people, but only one could survive. He knew it would be his people. His father had raised him to hate Israel, to hate the infidels in Europe and America that supported the invaders of his homeland. He looked at the board and thought how they were poised to wipe out all four million Jews and retake their homeland. He had planned it in detail, and the strategy was perfect.

The primary assault would be against Tel Aviv. This was the most important city strategically. It was Israel's commercial hub. Once that coastal city was secured, they would begin the expulsion and extermination of the Jewish population.

A subordinate came up and stood at attention. The general, without looking, asked, "What is it?"

The subordinate replied, "Sir, the gentleman is here to see you."

Mohammad nodded, sighed, and said, "Send him in." He sucked in a long breath of air.

After the subordinate sent him in, the man came in and stood silently as he waited for Mohammad to turn around. The general hated this man but knew he was a necessary evil. As much as he despised dealing with Westerners, he understood this man represented a huge conglomerate with seemingly unlimited financial resources, and it was this man's people that had made all this possible. It was this man's company that had helped unify the Muslim people and had brought the Chinese and Russian governments to their side. As much as he felt he should be thanking this man, there was always something about him, something slimy, that made Mohammad inexplicably suspicious of him. He slowly turned, forced a smile, and said, "Mr. Morphis, I thought you had already flown home. What has kept you here?"

Fred Morphis was an American. He was a middle-aged man with brown eyes and curly, salt and pepper hair. He stood five feet ten inches tall, had incredibly pale skin, and always seemed to wear some type of light-colored suit. Today, it was light gray and, along with his pale complexion, it made him look like a walking ghost, holding a black briefcase. He cleared his throat and said, "I was actually on my way to the airport when I was told there was a final detail I needed to get clarity on, so I was directed to come back."

The general nodded for him to continue, so Morphis said, "The plans you provided for my people outline your plans for the assault on Tel Aviv, but we didn't see anything for the planned invasion and destruction of Jerusalem."

Mohammad stared at him for a long moment. Then, he turned his back to him, looking back at the monitors again as he spoke, "There is no planned invasion, and we would never destroy Jerusalem. Our agreement was for the destruction of Israel. You have my word that will happen. Jerusalem is another matter."

Fred cleared his throat, set his briefcase down, and slowly approached the general, walking up beside him, standing on his left side. Fred said, "My people have provided enormous amounts of money and resources to make this happen. We have only asked for one thing, for Jerusalem to be destroyed."

Mohammad turned his head toward Morphis. "Our deal was Israel, not Jerusalem. My brothers will not destroy it. Jerusalem is our Holy City. It is more important to us than it is to the Jews or Christians. We will not drop a bomb on it if we can avoid it." He pointed to the monitors in front of them as he continued, "Their primary infrastructure is to the north. Their largest city is also to the north. Once that is taken, the rest is sure to fall swiftly, but we will take Jerusalem last, possibly without firing a shot, after everything else has been taken from them."

Frank looked at the monitors for a long moment. Then, he cleared his throat again as he spoke, "General, we had a deal, and my people expect you to honor it."

The general, still looking at the monitors, spoke again, "We will kill or expel the Jewish invaders as we agreed. We will wipe most of their cities and towns off the face of the earth, to be rebuilt for the new Muslim settlers, but we will not raise a hand against the Holy City."

Morphis looked at the monitors again and said, "If you do not comply, we will withdraw our support, and your coalition will fall apart. Do not forget. We are the ones who brought your people together. We are the ones who made all this possible."

The general turned to face him now and, with an intense glare, said, "Do not threaten me. We are grateful for your support, but you do not command us. You do not tell the army of Allah how it proceeds, where it goes, or what it does!"

Morphis stared back at him. Large beads of sweat began to appear on his large receding hairline as Mohammad continued, "We have your money, and your help is much appreciated." He, then, snapped his fingers, and two guards appeared almost instataneously. The general turned away and began to stare at the monitors again. He said, "Take Mr. Morphis to the airport. He has a flight to catch."

The guards motioned for Morphis to leave, so he slowly walked to his briefcase and picked it up. While looking at the general's back, Morphis said, "My people will not like this. They will feel betrayed."

Mohammad, continuing to stare at his monitors, replied, "If I were you, I would not speak again until you are out my country, or you may never get to leave."

With that, Morphis turned and left the room.

Chapter Fourteen

❧

✝el ΛUIU, ISRΛEL

Eve had called David, and surprisingly, he had agreed to come back to Israel. Once the Apostolate was gathered, David walked into the room. He was met with silence, icy stares, and suspicious looks. He looked around the room for a moment. Then, he sat in a chair at the opposite end of the table from the Apostle. To everyone's surprise, David spoke first, "I know you know about Ruth. I know I should have told you, but I loved her." He looked down, as if unsure of what else to say.

Job spoke next, "So you engage in something that is expressly forbidden, and you expect us to just forget and forgive, like it never happened?!"

David looked back up and said, "Forget, no, but forgive, yes." Following this statement, no one spoke, so David continued, "I thought that was what we were all about."

More silence.

David took a moment and looked around the room at each of them. Then, he said, "I'm not trying to make excuses. I'm not trying to say I was right. I know what we did was wrong, but I fell in love." David bowed his head again, thinking of the kindness this group had consistently given him. "I just wish I could have been there for her. I wish I could have saved her."

Job spoke again, "So, just like that, you are supposed to be one of us again?"

David looked up with surprising intensity and said, "I never stopped being one of us. I never stopped serving God. I wouldn't be here if I did."

Job, raising his voice now, said, "You lied to us! You betrayed us!"

David shouted back, "Lied, yes! But I never betrayed you!"

This caused looks of disappointment from the other men and women in the room.

A female member spoke next, "Lying is a form of betrayal. It creates an inability to trust. The two go together."

David sat back in his chair with his shoulders slumped and offered no argument. The Apostle stared at David. He wasn't sure what to say. He simply walked across the room, put his hand on David's shoulder, and said, "Forgiveness can, sometimes, be very difficult..." He looked around the room. Then, he continued, "For us all. But Jesus taught us it is essential. I trust you, and I believe God has sent you to us. We have little time now."

Job started to say something, but a stern look from the Apostle made him pause and sit back. The Apostle, then, looked at Eve and said, "I want you to take him to our most holy person."

Eve stared for a moment in disbelief. Then, she asked, "Are you sure? With everything going on?"

The Apostle looked at her again and said, "I want you to take some soldiers with you when you take him." He returned his gaze to David and said, "Time is precious. We have almost none, but I believe God wants you to go."

Eve motioned for David, and they left the room. As they walked down the narrow hall, David asked, "Where are we going?"

Eve, still looking straight ahead, replied, "He wants you to go to the holiest person on the planet, a person we believe is closer to God than anyone who is currently alive."

David considered it a moment. He tried to think of who this might be. Then, he asked, "I'm going to meet the Pope?"

Chapter Fifteen

BEIJING, CHINA

The Chairman was addressing the supreme council, and she was furious. She pounded her fist into the table with surprising strength and noise as she shouted, "I won't tolerate a failure of this magnitude! All the time and energy we have spent, our entire reserve resources!"

The impeccably dressed men and women around the table, representing most of the major nations in the world, were stiff and stared straight ahead, afraid to move or speak. This was, after all, a woman who could have anyone killed for any reason and had shown she would do so, if provoked.

After calming herself, she said, "This is the end. Our decades-long efforts have led us to this place. We have been incredibly successful." She took a deep breath, calming herself further. Then, she spoke again, "We have neutralized the Christians, the U.S. and, in the process, the rest of Europe. With great expenditure of resources, influence, and all our financial capital, we have united the Asian powers with the Middle Eastern countries, and now we are ready to squash Israel."

She stopped and looked around the room. The rest were still too scared to speak. She continued, "We have the child. The child! He has been delivered unto us, and we will raise him in our image. The only thing left is to ensure the destruction of Jerusalem. Despite our efforts, the Muslim army will focus on Tel-Aviv. Therefore, Jerusalem's future still remains uncertain."

She looked around the room, as if waiting for someone to speak, but every person in the room just stared straight ahead. She got up and began to walk around the room as she spoke, "We are being tested. We are being challenged. We have to show we will do anything for our master, to secure his earthly throne." She finished a circle around the table, sat back in her chair at the head of the table, and then spoke in a low tone, "I want all our people called home. Imps, every-one, bring them all in."

With this, the men and women in the room slowly turned their heads in her direction. She was a vain woman. She loved her power and relished the fear she saw in their eyes when they looked at her. She took it in as she spoke confidently, "The day is close at hand. It is not a coincidence. The day approaches at the same time as Jerusalem's destruction. I am going to take the child to have him anointed. Cain, our master's earthly tool, will command the rest of you, and you will destroy Jerusalem. Once it is destroyed, we can offer the ashes to our allies after they destroy the rest of Israel. Over the next few days, the prophesies of generations will come to pass, and our dominion over Earth will begin."

Chapter Sixteen

WEST VIRGINIA, UNITED STATES

David realized he wasn't meeting the Pope when the plane landed in America. They had been driving for several hours. The mountains were imposing, and the roads were winding and narrow. The minivan was at its seven-person capacity. David was in the front passenger seat, with Eve sitting behind him. One soldier drove, and four more sat silently. The van jolted as they hit a large pothole. Annoyed, Eve said, "I've lost count. Can you try not to hit anymore?"

The man shook his head in frustration and said, "Yes, ma'am, I'll try, but they're everywhere."

Soon, they were off the paved road and driving on a dirt road. Amazingly, there seemed to be less potholes on the dirt road than there had been on paved one.

David asked, "Can you tell me where we are now?"

Eve replied, "West Virginia."

David spun his head around to face her and repeated, "West Virginia. Is that even a state?"

The van jolted, and the driver said, "Sorry. I couldn't dodge that one."

David returned his gaze to the front windshield and asked, "How much farther?"

Eve replied, "Not far. We will be there soon. She is expecting us."

"She?" asked David.

"She," replied Eve. Then, she continued, "We believe she is closer to God than anyone currently alive. She has been given the gift of prophesy, and numerous soldiers have seen her in visions. We believe she has great wisdom. She has been a source of guidance for us for many years. She is getting very old now."

"How old?" David asked.

"No one knows. My guess is over one hundred, but we don't ask her those kinds of questions."

The van finally came to a stop outside of an old home. As everyone got out, David stretched, feeling the jetlag, and looked around. The home was very plain, and it looked worn. It had old white siding, a tin roof, and a sagging front porch that looked like it was drooping and was going to fall away from the house. The white picket fence was in bad need of repair, and the gate had fallen off its hinges and was lying nearby, propped up on the side of the fence. It reminded David of a farm. There were several dogs and cats lying around on the porch and in the yard. He could hear pigs in the distance, and chickens were everywhere, pecking and strutting about. As they approached the opening in the fence that led up to the dirty sidewalk, they stopped. Everyone began removing their heavy boots and setting them aside.

As Eve removed her boots, she looked at David and said, "David, take off your boots."

David looked at her in disbelief and asked incredulously, "Why?!"

One of the soldiers replied, "Because you're about to step on holy ground."

As they entered the home, David felt the floorboards sagging beneath him. The low ceiling had visible cracks, and the off-white walls were covered with pictures; many were black and white. The floor was covered with old, cracked, and yellowing linoleum.

Across the small living room, sitting on a worn-out sofa, was a small, African-American woman. She said, "Come in. Come on in."

They slowly filled the small living room.

She squinted to look at them and said, "Which of you is David?"

David awkwardly stepped forward and said, "I am, uh, that would be me." He was feeling very strange about this place and this woman. This was nothing like he had expected.

She motioned with her right arm and said, "Well, come on over here and let me get a better look at you."

David slowly approached her and took in her appearance. She looked as if she was barely five feet tall. She was very skinny and petite. Her dark eyes looked hollow and sunk into her head. Her hair was white and was pulled back tightly on her head. Her cheeks looked shallow and sunken, and her mouth had almost no lips. But she had a warm, welcoming smile.

When David got in front of her, she reached out and took his hands into her own. Her hands were surprisingly warm. From her seated position, she stared up at David and looked him over. She laughed and said, "Well, so you are the one I have been hearing about. My eyes aren't what they used to be, but for all you have to do, I thought you would be a bigger man."

David gave her a surprised look, unsure of what to say. Then, she started to laugh. Still holding his hands, she said, "It's okay. He is a miracle worker, so it really doesn't matter." Her laugh slowly subsided, and she gazed directly into his eyes and said, "You are the last one."

David, again, didn't know what to say, so he simply asked, "Ma'am?"

She said, "Many have come before you, but none will come after you. The end of days is upon us, and you are the last one."

David spun his head around to look at Eve, who just stared at him. He spun his head back and repeated, "Last one?"

She laughed again and said, "Now, you didn't think you were the first one, did you?"

David stared blankly, as she let go of his hands.

She patted the seat on the old couch to her right and said, "Sit, sit."

David did as he was told.

She shifted in her seated position with a groan and said, "Your powers. Did you think you were the first?" David shook his head as she continued, "There have been others over the years. God's chosen ones."

David repeated, "Chosen?"

She continued, "David, you have to understand that many are called but few are chosen. You were chosen for a reason. I have been seeing you in my visions of late. I have been expecting you, but I didn't know you were already here till a few months ago." She hit her own leg, and her face became animated as she said, "What a story! An unbeliever, a self-proclaimed atheist. What God can do with so little and make so much. Whew!"

David just continued to stare. He was still unsure of what to say or how to act. He cleared his throat and asked, "Can you tell me anything about the others, the ones that came before me?"

She said, "Well, they all served a purpose, just as you do. Many chose to serve God, as you do now. They each had a role and came to carry a certain title. All were put here to do as God commanded. When the time comes, you will have your chance to as well."

David repeated, "I will have my chance?"

She nodded. "Yes, you still have free will. When the time comes, you have to make sure you are ready, ready to listen."

David asked, "When will that time be? What will I need to do?"

She closed her eyes and took a couple of deep breaths. She opened her eyes again and said, "I have nothing else. What I have given you is all there is."

Disappointed, David said, "Maybe I can come and see you again sometime?"

"No," she replied flatly.

David repeated, "No?"

She smiled and said, "I will be crossing over soon. My time is almost up." She grabbed her cane, which was lying next to her, and groaned as she came to her feet, revealing a deeply hunched-over posture.

David quickly stood beside her and said, "I'm sorry. I didn't know you were sick."

She laughed and said, "I'm not sick. It's just my time. We all have one, and mine is almost here. I have eight kids, twelve grandkids, twenty-seven great-grandkids, and four great-great-grandkids. I think I've left a small mark on the world. I was hoping to get to meet my next great-great-grandchild. She is due to be born soon." She let out a weary breath and continued, "But it's not looking good. I'm sorry you came all this way, and I couldn't give you more, but I never know when he is going to speak to me, and what I have told you is all I have been given."

David nodded and, feeling some despair, took a couple of steps toward the door. Then, he started to feel strange. He could feel something, like an energy in the room. He could feel emotion wash over him. He knew it was the Holy Spirit. He closed his eyes and prayed, "Please, Lord, give me something. I need something more. I don't know what I am supposed to do."

Suddenly, he heard a noise. One of the soldiers gasped, and David spun around. The old woman's cane had fallen to the floor. To everyone's astonishment, she was standing perfectly upright. The hunch was gone, and with the perfect posture, her eyes sprang wide open. She looked at David with an intense stare and said, "My sheep will know my voice."

David asked, "What?"

She repeated, "He said, 'My sheep will know my voice.' Soon the bell will ring. The trumpet will blow." She hesitated, as if unsure of what she was hearing. Then, she looked upward and said, "Run!"

David looked confused. He looked back at Eve again, who was staring intently at the old woman. David spun his head back toward her again. She said, "When you hear his voice, don't you walk. You run! Do you hear me, David? You run!"

David looked like a confused child, but he said, "I hear you. I hear you."

After speaking those last words and hearing David's reply, the old woman slouched over again, and without her cane, she fell toward the floor. David instinctively caught her with his power. As he raised his right hand up, he was keeping her from falling, and with lightning speed, Eve ran forward and grabbed her, helping her to sit back on the couch. The old woman, stunned by the experience, said, "Now this is something you don't get to see every day." As Eve helped her, she pulled Eve's ear to her mouth and said, "There is a reason you didn't die. You still have work to do. It will be revealed soon. Be ready to act quickly when he calls on you."

Chapter Seventeen

WASHINGTON, D.C.

The President had easily won reelection. The celebration had been going on long into the night. The President should have been happy, but he wasn't. His hand had begun hurting earlier in the night from too many hard handshakes, and the pain had grown progressively worse. Desperate for some time alone, he stole away a moment to himself. He looked around the banquet at the mass of people, ladies in fine gowns and men in tuxedos. He had shaken most of their hands, as his sore hand and wrist attested, maybe a few too many.

He had gotten a glass of punch and was attempting to have a much-needed break in the corner of the room. He was drinking with his left hand, which felt awkward, but the pain in his right hand would not allow him to grip the fine glass goblet. He loved the punch. He always looked forward to it anytime there was a party. He knew the chef that oversaw the cooking staff had served five administrations now, and many of her items were very popular with the Washington elite, the punch being one of them.

He sipped again and let a slight smile pass his lips. For all the discussion around her famous items, he had discovered the secrets were normally very simple. As a man that liked to have midnight snacks often, he had come to know the chef more closely than most of his predecessors. She had confided the punch was simply orange sherbet, pineapple juice, club soda, and her secret ingredient: Sprite. The smile was a welcome respite from everything he had been enduring.

As the smile faded, his mind quickly went back to the enormous weight of the problems he faced. He continued to feel trapped, and he was watching helplessly as the entire world was being turned upside down. He thought of Young, of all the people he seemed to have aligned with him. He was feeling more isolated now than ever. The head of his Secret Service detail approached him. Observing the look on the President's face, he asked, "You okay, sir?"

The President looked back at him for a moment. Then, he said, "Yes, fine, Bays."

Jeremy Bays was one of the youngest men to ever head a Secret Service detail, taking over the presidential detail at only twenty-four. He got started at twenty-one and was moved up in only three and a half years. Now with more than a decade of experience, he was known as an incredibly thorough man, who was a well-known workaholic, which accounted for such a meteoric rise in such a short time. The President knew him as a charismatic man who made friends easily, and he and the President had bonded during his first term.

Bays was 6'2" with hazel eyes, and he wore his sandy blond hair closely cropped and spiked on top, a hairstyle he had stubbornly clung to since the 1990s, when his mother did his hair. His son, Evan, was commonly known to be his world, but his wife, Tara, was pregnant with twin girls, and the President knew things would change at home for him soon.

"How's Evan?" asked the President.

"Fine, sir," came the reply.

"He anxious about the girls?" asked the President.

Bays replied with a light laugh, "I don't think he knows to be yet, but he's getting ready to get two new siblings, so his Christmas gift budget is getting ready to take a big hit."

Bays' humor was well known, and right now, it was appreciated. As the President's smile faded, Bays said, "I just wanted to check on you, sir. We will be over there when you're ready. We'll make sure no one gets over here, so you can have another moment alone."

The President smiled and nodded as Bays moved several feet away. He raised the cup back to his lips again and realized his hand was shaking. It was as if he could feel a weight descending on him in the dark corner of the room. He stopped and let his eyes take a turn around the room. Suddenly, the familiar faces looked dark and gloomy, and the darkness seemed to overtake the entire room. As he slowly scanned the dance floor in the half-dark room, he saw faces looking back at him suspiciously, darkly. He began to feel an evil presence creep around him, as yellow eyes seemed to be staring at him. The darkness seemed to be almost suffocating.

As he wiped sweat from his forehead, the Secret Service agents looked on, as if oblivious to everything he was seeing. He lowered the punch in his shaking hand and turned away, toward the corner. A feeling of loneliness overtook him like he had never felt before. He suddenly felt under attack and all alone. Without thinking, he cried out in a low voice, "Please, God, please! I need to know I'm not alone."

"You're not alone."

He spun around, spilling punch on the floor by his feet as he did. There was a young woman standing in front of him.

"There are quite a few people here," she said with a smile.

He looked around, shocked for a moment. Then, he took her in — long, flowing, blondish-brown hair, brown eyes, a round face with high cheekbones, and surprisingly no make-up, which told him instantly she was not from Washington.

Still somewhat in shock, the President mumbled, "Sorry. I didn't see you there."

The woman confidently extended a hand and said, "No need to apologize, Mr. President. I just appreciate the chance to meet you in person."

The President smiled and nodded, as he wondered how she got past the Secret Service detail. Still somewhat off-guard, he slowly extended a weary right hand. To his surprise, she gently took the punch from his hand, set it down on a nearby table, and shook his left hand. "I'm sorry, but with all the handshaking tonight, I thought you might appreciate the chance to use the other hand."

When she shook, she shook with both hands, and the moment their hands touched and she wrapped his hand in her hands, he felt something warm, something very comforting. In that moment, he felt his heart slow and his mind calm. It reminded him of being comforted by his mother when he was a small child. The feeling disarmed him, and for a moment, he just enjoyed the sensation. Then, realizing his hand was still inside her hands, he jerked it away and said, "Nice to meet you, um…"

"Wood. Bethany Wood. Very nice to get to meet you, sir."

"Wood," he repeated. "I don't recognize the name."

She smiled and said, "I am with the Christian Coalition."

He had heard the Christian Coalition had been in town and were making another motion for prayer in schools. For a moment, a silence settled between them. Then, she asked, "So you were saying you were alone?"

The President laughed nervously, somewhat embarrassed, as he replied, "No, not really."

She looked at him like she could read his mind. Somehow, with her knowing look, he knew she knew he was lying and, against his initial judgment, he felt the need to be honest with her, "Sometimes, I think we all feel that way. I seem to a lot lately. As a Christian, I would imagine recent events have made you feel more isolated than in the past?" She spoke with a soft confidence he was not used to.

"No, I don't feel alone or isolated, but I do feel the need for prayer. When darkness descends the way it has recently, I feel we should all pray. Satan and his demons are on the loose, and we need to unite." The President smiled nervously and tried to cover his serious-ness with humor. He forced a smile and said, "I am seeing a lot of demons these days."

Wood softly touched his arm and leaned in as she said, "They are getting bolder now. It's going to get worse. This nation was once a Christian nation. It can be again. There have been presidents in our past that united us and put God at the forefront of our country. What we need is a president that will do that again — get our people united and seeking God. You could be this person. Then, these demons will have no choice but to return to where they came from."

The President sensed the seriousness in her tone, but it all seemed so overwhelming right now.

Wood, then, asked, "Do you understand the concept of interces-sory prayer?"

The President had heard the term, but in truth, didn't understand it, so he shook his head.

She continued, "God said, 'When two or more are gathered in my name, then I am in their midst.' There are angels to combat these demons."

Trying to comprehend what she was saying, the President asked, "Are you saying that prayer will unleash them?"

Wood replied, "They are already engaged in warfare for us. When we pray, we battle as well. We all have to pray. The more of us that pray, the more God will allow them to help us. As things stand now, they are still here, but they are forced to operate in the shadows."

The President felt comfort in her words, but worry still hung over him. He tried to force a smile. Then, he said, "Well, I know God won't give us more than we can handle."

She shook her head, still smiling, and said, "Well, that's not exactly accurate."

Surprised, he said, "But I thought … I mean … I have always heard…"

She interrupted, "What the Bible actually says is, he will not give you more than you can handle without him. But if you choose to try to carry those burdens alone, then you will definitely have more than you can handle."

The President listened to her intently, trying to take it all in, but this was so different from what he had always heard. He asked, "I'm sorry, but are you sure that's correct?"

She replied, "Maybe you should read the Bible and learn for yourself. There are examples in many places. Take Daniel and the lions' den, the Hebrew boys in the fiery furnace, or Peter after the Pentecost. The time is rapidly approaching where you will have to make some hard decisions. The nation and your people need you."

A hand suddenly appeared on his shoulder. "Sir, several of the guests are asking for you."

The President spun around to see Bays in front of him. Surprised, he said, "Yes, um, please have someone clean up the punch on the floor."

Bays looked at him puzzled and asked, "Sir?"

The President motioned around his feet and said, "The pun—"

The floor was totally dry. Then, he looked back at Bays and said, "I could have sworn I spilled some as I turned to speak to Ms. Wood."

Bays, still looking puzzled, asked, "To whom, sir?"

The President turned as he replied, "To Ms…"

No one was there. He looked around to see where she'd gone but could not find any sign of her. He quickly scanned the room, trying to find her. He turned to Bays and said, "The woman I was talking to, where did she go?"

Bays looked nervous and replied, "I'm sorry, sir, but I don't see a woman."

The President turned again, trying to find her in the crowded room, but he couldn't see her. He turned and slowly walked back into the crowded banquet. As he reached the crowd, he turned one last time and saw the glass of punch setting on the table, right where she'd placed it.

Chapter Eighteen

BEIJING, CHINA

Judas was nervous. He missed the hoodie that had become a sort of mental protection for his appearance. He stepped off the elevator as people looked up, and while some quickly looked away, others just stared in disbelief at this horribly disfigured man. He had gotten used to it, but missed his hood, which offered some deflection against these looks.

As he approached the secretary's desk, he noticed a pained look as her eyes took him in. She quickly looked down at her computer, attempting to appear busy, as she said, "Yes, um, she is ready for you."

He silently walked past her and into the office. As he entered, he was surprised to see Cain sitting in the other chair, facing her desk. He had been here before, but no matter how many times he came, he never failed to notice all the luxurious accommodations she had everywhere. There was a fine mahogany desk with high-backed leather chairs. The view from the window was a better look at the city than any tourist would ever get. He turned his gaze to Cain. He felt very uncomfortable around him. He had not seen him since Brazil. The Chairman, motioning to the empty chair, said, "You may sit."

Judas moved to the chair and sat down, the leather chair making a loud noise as he did. Cain looked over at Judas with disgust and asked, "What is this thing doing here? Why isn't he dead? All he has done is continue to fail us and our master."

To Judas's surprise, the Chairman was quiet and looked toward him for a response, but he simply let his head hang toward the floor. The Chairman looked at Cain. Then, she looked at Judas again, ignoring Cain's comment as she spoke, "The time is upon us. I have called everyone home. We have bankrupted this mighty company, but everything is proceeding as planned; however, the Muslims will not attack Jerusalem, so we will have to do it. Our intelligence says the Israeli army will be putting every last man, woman, and child old enough to hold a weapon in front of the massive Muslim army assembling to attack Tel Aviv. The Muslims want to try to conquer Jerusalem without destroying it, and we cannot allow that to happen. Our master has long made clear his plans for Jerusalem's destruction, which will pave the way for our future leader to sit on his earthly throne. This is where Judas will come in."

Nodding in his direction and turning the conversation back to him, the Chairman said, "It's true. He has failed us, but I will decide when and how he pays for his failures. I believe he has one last task to perform for us. Once that is complete, I will let him die with dignity, but that is a matter for us to discuss later."

Cain looked at Judas in disgust. Then, he turned and shifted his gaze to the Chairman. She continued, "We are transporting every last resource and all our people to the desert outside of Jerusalem. I have made it clear that you are in charge of this effort. The Israeli defense forces will be totally focused on the massive Muslim army that is advancing on Tel Aviv. Once they all march out of Jerusalem, you will move in with our people and destroy the city. Leave no building standing. Leave no one alive."

Cain was silent. The Chairman patiently waited for a reply. After an uncomfortably long silence, he asked, "And what will you be doing with this worthless man while I am doing our master's bidding?"

She replied, "We will anoint the child. This is not the way we planned to do it, but this situation is moving too fast to take our time. Once he is anointed and Jerusalem is destroyed, our Muslim friends will let us walk him through the ashes. Then, we will be ready to start the process that will lead to him and us setting up our master's earthly throne and usher in his return. Jehovah gave the Christians Jesus, and now it is our turn. Now it is our time."

Cain stared at her long and hard. Then, he asked, "And David?"

The Chairman replied, "In the wind, as far as we know. You finish this last task for us, and as a reward, I will let you handpick as many of our people as you want, and you can spend as long as you want, hunting him down to the ends of the earth."

A smile crossed Cain's face, and he quickly stood as he spoke, "The next time we meet, it will be in Jerusalem, after I have destroyed the city."

The Chairman nodded and said, "The Christians will most likely try to mobilize what is left of their pathetic movement. We have neutralized them to the point that they are not a real threat, but be ready to wipe them out as well."

In Cain's mind, this made perfect sense. Suddenly, it all came together for him. Satan was working through this woman, and his doubts about her were proving unfounded. She was their leader, and though he had not always trusted her, he had always trusted Satan. Now, he could see everything coming together as it had been predicted.

Giving her an approving look, Cain smiled, and the Chairman allowed a thin smile to appear on her lips as well. She and Cain never agreed on anything, but they both could feel the demons in the air. Satan's power was all around them. She allowed herself to take in the joy of what she had accomplished. She gave Cain an approving look and, as if reading his mind, said, "The Christian Bible prophesied all we are going to begin here together. Let's make sure we deliver all the death and destruction their book of Revelation predicted."

Suddenly, Cain beamed as he said, "Consider it already done!" Cain had never looked at her this way. For the first time, he looked at her as the leader she knew she was. She gave him another approving look, and he turned, without speaking to or acknowledging Judas, and he left the room.

The Chairman, then, looked at Judas. His head was still hung. As he slowly raised his head, she stared at him and said, "I know you prefer wearing hoods when you can, but there was a reason I told you not to wear them anymore. I wanted you to feel the shame of your appearance. I wanted you to feel the shame of who you are. I wanted to kill you after you failed me again, but there is a reason you are still here." She let that statement hang in the air for a moment as Judas gave her a soft stare. He was a broken man now. She continued, "You were defeated by your son. Then, you allowed your other son to kill our best unit. When we discovered what happened, I planned to have you killed when you returned, but Satan has another plan for you."

She paused to give him a minute to speak. He seemed like a defeated animal to her, like some pathetic dog she would see on the street. When he didn't speak, she continued, "I have allowed you to visit the child and be involved in his care for one reason … because you are his grandfather. Satan wants you there when we dedicate him. I have selected the best of our men and women. They will accompany us to the holy site, and we will make his dedication now. As his earthly grandfather, you will give him to Satan. You will hand him over and watch his rebirth to our master."

For the first time, a slight smile passed Judas's lips.

The Chairman continued, "Once this is accomplished, I will kill you, as you will have served your purpose. If you do everything to my specifications, I will execute you myself and let you die with some semblance of dignity."

Judas stared for a moment. Then, he nodded. This was the best he could hope for, and he knew it was more than he deserved.

Chapter Nineteen

✝ΕL ΑUΙU, ΙSRΑΕL

U pon their return to the compound, David and Eve were met with chaos. As they entered the old stone walls, there was an unusual hustle and bustle of activity. A man with a barrel was burning some things, but David couldn't make out what it was. Someone came running by and bumped into one of the men with them but didn't stop and kept running. Shouts could be heard everywhere. David looked in another direction and could see guns and ammunition being stacked out in the open. As they moved inside, David entered the room to find the Apostolate already assembled. The stress the Apostle was under was obvious from the look on his face.

David said, "There is a lot of activity going on."

The Apostle just nodded and motioned for David to sit. As David sat, the Apostle asked, "Were you able to get answers from her?"

David stared for a moment and nodded as he spoke, "Some, but there are still a few things I need to figure out."

The Apostle, stone-faced now and feeling his patience strained, said, "I would imagine there will always be some things you will need to figure out, David. None of us go through life with all the answers.

I need to know if you are with us now or not because we are out of time."

David and Job looked at each other with an intense stare, but after a moment, both turned toward the Apostle as he said, "Yes, I think this is where God wants me to be."

With this, the Apostle sat back in his chair for a moment, as if lost in thought. He turned his gaze back to David and said, "David, it is coming, and fast now. The Muslim army, over a million strong, is assembling to march on Israel. Their target will be Tel Aviv, which is Israel's largest city and commercial hub. Israel is not giving up, and they have activated the home guard. Every man, woman, and child will be marching to meet this army outside of Tel Aviv."

David looked at him, wide-eyed, as the realization of this settled on him.

The Apostle continued, "The Satanists want Jerusalem destroyed. They believe the destruction of Jerusalem will signal the beginning of their ascendancy to domination of the Earth. With the fighting at Tel Aviv, Jerusalem will be unprotected against the Satanist forces. We are marching there to protect the people and the city."

David stared for another moment. Then, he said, "You speak like this is Armageddon, but why now? Why, after all this time, are they making this move?"

The Apostle looked at Job. Then, he looked back at David as he spoke, "They believe the Anti-Christ has been delivered unto the Earth."

David stared in disbelief. The Apostle looked at Job again. Then, he looked back at David, yet again, as he said, "David, we can't delay anymore. We need you to be with us. Our people will be outnumbered and outgunned. I believe God wants you to be with us, and you may be our only hope for survival."

David nodded as he stared off in thought.

The Apostle continued, "The Satanists have a child, a small infant, only a couple of months old. They believe this child is the prophesied Anti-Christ they have waited for…for centuries."

David continued to stare.

The Apostle said, "David, if you are going to be with us, there can be no secrets between us, nothing unsaid. It is for that reason I have to tell you this now. That child is your son."

David was stunned. He felt himself fall back in his chair, as he continued to stare off blankly. He had a son?! He couldn't believe it. Ruth had been pregnant?! How could he have not known? His head spun as he felt emotions he could not describe. He heard Job speak, "We don't know what this child could grow to be or what he is capable of."

The room broke out into a frenzy of conversation. David just sat, trying to take it all in, but he could hear the comments swirling around the room: "The child is an abomination." "We need to kill him." "He is the Anti-Christ!"

With this, David felt his blood boil, and the room began to softly shake. It felt like an earthquake, and suddenly, everyone fell silent, and all eyes fell on David, who was gripping the table with white knuckles with an intense stare on his face. His face was flush with anger, and he slowly spun his head around with gritted teeth, looking at each of them. The room began to shake even more, and the Apostle screamed, "David!"

David looked up with a blank stare. Then, slowly, the shaking subsided, and the room returned to normal. David stared directly into the Apostle's eyes. The Apostle, in a soft voice said, "David, we need you. We need you with us."

David didn't respond, just continued to stare at him. After an awkward moment, David spoke surprisingly softly, "No. I have to go and get my son. That is all that matters now." Everything seemed to be happening so fast. David was still processing the shock of it all.

Job, incredulous, said, "And forsake the God you swore to serve?! Forget all else?!"

David felt his anger begin to flare again. He started to speak, but then, he felt a strong hand on his right arm. "David, this is it! This is what God spared me to do. This is what he kept me alive for."

David, still seething, spun his head slowly to his right, and his eyes met Eve's. The look of determination he saw there gave him pause. She returned his intense stare with one of her own. This made David stop, and for a moment anyway, he felt he had to listen.

Eve, sensing she had seconds to convince him, went to a squatting position, and with her hand still on David's forearm, said, "Think about it. I should not be here. I should have died with my men." Her eyes welled up with tears, and as they began to stream down her cheeks, she confessed, "I wanted to die. I felt I deserved to die with my men. I couldn't understand why God did not let me die with them. The doctors told me I should not have lived, but something kept my body alive, kept me from dying. I have been so angry, and I have carried that anger ever since I woke up in that hospital, but I understand now. This is why I didn't." The tears continued to stream. "David, you can't be in two places at once. This is what God has for me. This is what I have to do. I am meant to save your son, to return him to you safe and sound."

David was undecided, everything was happening so fast.

Then, Eve, her face wet with tears and her body shaking, said, "I vow it! I swear it! With every breath in my body and with every ounce of my strength, as God is my witness, if you give me the chance, I will rescue your son and deliver him into your arms."

David felt himself soften. For a moment, he closed his eyes. He couldn't hear it in words, but he began to sense she was right. This was what God intended. He heard the Apostle's voice, "David, we need you. I have no idea what we will be marching into, but the Satanists have played their hand. They are sensing a final victory, and we cannot let them take Jerusalem. We will be marching to meet them."

As David pushed himself up and out of his chair slowly, all eyes were still on him. He looked at Eve. "Okay. You go." He stood, grabbed her shoulders, and pulled her close. David's intense stare gave Eve pause. He looked into her eyes and said, "I'm trusting you, trusting you with my son's life. You bring him to me and only me. Understand?"

Eve blinked away tears, nodded quickly, and repeated, "I will bring him to you."

David slowly looked around the room and said, "I will go with you." Then, he looked at the Apostle and said, "I don't know what I will do yet. I need to pray and seek guidance and find out what God wants me to do."

The Apostle seemed to accept this. He looked at Eve for a moment. Then, he instructed, "Go. Take what soldiers you can find and go. Bring him back to us."

Eve nodded, spun, and left the room.

The Apostle gave David a grave, solemn look. He took a deep breath, as if already exhausted, and said, "David, I have called everyone here. I sent word for all our people and anyone that wanted to help us to come home. Everything the Satanists are doing is clear to us, and they believe we are powerless to stop them. But I believe this is God's design. Nothing happens without Him. I believe we are destined to face them, and the time is upon us."

He rose and moved to a door that opened to a small, stone balcony. As he exited, the rest of the Apostolate and David followed him. As David saw the spectacle, he gasped for a moment. There was a sea of people stretching back as far as the eye could see. Both men and women, old and young. He knew his old friends Jeremiah, Moses, and Ester were in there somewhere. He knew he couldn't find them now, but he said a prayer in his mind for them and for all the people he was looking at now.

The Apostle turned, looked at David with pride, and said, "This is what our God can do. There is a power in these people, and we will not give up now. These people, this army of God, will march in defense of Jerusalem."

Chapter Twenty

WASHINGTON, D.C.

It was late. Most of the White House staff were either gone or asleep at this hour. The President looked at his desk, full of papers, full of work. He looked up at the television on the wall. The volume was muted, but he could see what was happening. The coverage was unprecedented. The reporter was on the ground with an army that was reported to be over a million men. The reporter was interviewing a man who had walked over a hundred miles to take part in the Jihad that was going to rid the Arabian Peninsula of the Jewish nation and all its people in one, grand battle. American reaction was mixed, with most siding with Israel, but a strong minority said this was "none of our business," and they demanded that America stay out of it.

Regardless of the debate, his administration was continuing to be silent on the matter. Disgusted, the President grabbed the remote, turned off the television, stepped away from his desk, and began to pace around the room. He felt so helpless and lost. He was a broken, defeated man, and he didn't see any way out. He had gotten a good man killed, and he knew that man's blood was on his hands alone. He thought about the people, how he had let them down.

When he was first elected, he'd had such high hopes. He thought about his daughter, his only child, and his responsibility to keep his little girl safe. But they had perfectly blocked his every move. He was left with no other options. He walked to the window and watched as the rain poured down hard. He felt something on his face, and as he reached up and touched it, he realized it was a tear. This surprised him. He couldn't remember the last time he had cried.

Suddenly, as he looked into the storm, he felt the storm in his own life, and he thought about his failure as a man and as a president who couldn't protect his own people. The weight of all of it began to press down hard on him. He felt overwhelmed with sorrow and grief. He suddenly felt weak. His knees felt like they would buckle, so he gave in and collapsed upon them.

As he fell to his knees and felt tears streaming down his cheeks, he put his shaking hands together and raised them. Then, slowly, he looked up into the storm and said in a hoarse, shaky voice, "Please, God, please. You know my heart. I am desperate. I am not a praying man. I know you know that, and I'm not asking for myself. I'm asking for my people. I'm surrounded, Lord, surrounded by enemies on all sides."

He began to sob. As his chest heaved, he wasn't sure what else to say. He thought about Young. He was like a demon. There were demons all around him now. He looked back up and begged, "Send me an angel, Lord! Send me an angel to help me! Please, Lord!"

At that moment, there was a knock at the door. Surprised, he shakily came to his feet and staggered to his desk. After quickly looking for tissue and not finding any, he wiped his face with his hand. Then, he turned his head to the right and wiped his face with his right shirt sleeve. Afterward, he said, "Come in."

As his daughter entered, wearing a housecoat and slippers, she asked, "Dad, you still up?"

The President blew out a long breath and replied, "Yes, honey. Why aren't you asleep?"

She didn't answer. She walked to the front of his desk and sat down in front of him, crossing her legs. She took a long breath of her own and asked, "Are you ever going to talk to me? Like we used to?"

The President didn't respond.

She smiled and continued, "I remember, when I was a little girl, I used to think, My daddy tells me everything. I used to think, My daddy is the most powerful man in the whole world. Now you are, but somehow, you are not you anymore."

The President replied, "I'm sorry I disappoint you."

As she looked at him with a calm and considerate expression, she said, "No, you haven't disappointed me. I love you." She leaned forward. "I know you better than anyone besides Mom, who you have shut out, and this isn't you. She went on another of her international trips because she can't talk to you anymore. This isn't you at all."

He looked at her for a moment. He couldn't help wondering where his little girl had gone. This was a woman he was talking to. He used to think, when she was grown, he would see his wife in her, but he saw himself in her, too. She had a softness he had come to know in his wife, but he could sense his own inner strength in the woman that sat in front of him. He said, "You don't know. There is no way you could understand what I'm up against."

She replied, "Then, explain it to me. Have we really drifted that far apart? What could you possibly be up against that you can't handle? Daddy, you are the president of the United States. The people just reelected you to another term. What could you possibly have to be worried about? What could possibly be troubling you so?"

He just stared at her.

She tried again, "Please, Daddy, talk to me."

He stared for a moment. Then, in spite of himself, he relented. He was desperate to share this burden with someone, but he knew he couldn't tell her everything. He looked off as he spoke, "I am under attack from every side. There are people here that wield enormous power, a power I cannot control, and they will do anything…" He stopped and leveled his gaze at her. "Anything to ensure they get what they want."

She looked at him, puzzled, and asked, "What could they possibly threaten you with?"

He didn't respond. He only rose, moved to the window, and stared out at the storm.

Realization dawned in her eyes, and she said, "It's me, isn't it? They threatened me."

Still silent, he continued to stare out the window. She rose and moved to him. She stood directly behind him and said, "You feel helpless, don't you? You feel backed into a corner because they threatened me."

The President, still speechless, just continued to stare.

His daughter said, "So what did they threaten you with? What did they say they were going to do?"

The President wouldn't respond. He had already said too much.

She continued, "Dad, you have to stand up to these people, whoever they are. You can't give in to people like that."

The President, still staring out the window, felt his lips quiver and said in a frustrated voice, "Don't you think I know that?! Don't you think I understand what I'm doing?! I've given up my people, the people I swore on the Bible I would protect. I have given them up because I can't imagine a world where you are not in it, a world where I don't do everything I possibly can to keep you safe." He was fighting back tears. Just the thought of losing his little girl was more than he could bear.

His daughter said, "Dad, look at me."

He didn't turn.

She grabbed his shoulders with surprising strength and spun him toward her, forcing him to look at her. She repeated, "Look at me!"

He looked into her eyes and saw a strength in them, a determination.

She said, "Dad, I am not a little girl anymore. I am a woman, and I can take care of myself. You are my father, and I know you are better than this."

He looked at her, but he could feel fear gripping him. He kept thinking of losing her and knowing, if he did, he would forever lose himself. If that happened, he knew he could never live with it, and it would kill him. He looked down at the floor.

She said, "Dad, we have to stand up to this. You have to stand up to this. You are better than this. Our family is better than this."

He raised his head again and said, "You have no idea what we are up against. No idea." She looked at him again, puzzled.

And he continued, "These are not just men. There are forces you can't imagine." He expected her to move away from him now and either leave or sit down, but she just stared at him. There was silence for a long moment. He didn't know what else to say. He was exhausted. Finally, he muttered, "I am surrounded by demons … all the time." He looked her in the eye again and muttered in a low voice, "They're everywhere."

She continued to stare. She finally turned, walked away from him, and started toward the door.

He regretted talking to her at all. He was so weak now. He didn't understand why he had even told her any of this. He hoped she would go to bed and rest. One of them should be able to get some sleep.

To his surprise, she moved past the door, to a bookcase, selected a book, came back to his desk, and laid the book down on top of it. She looked at him angrily and asked, "So when was the last time you opened this up!?"

He slowly walked to the desk and realized it was the Bible he had laid his hand on for his swearing in ceremony. It belonged to his grandmother and had been in his family for generations. He looked back at his daughter now and realized it wasn't anger he saw; it was determination. He had never seen her look like this before.

She demanded, "Answer me! When did you look at this last?"

He honestly couldn't remember.

She said, "You made sure I grew up in church, remember? You promised Grandma I would be there every week, and you kept your promise."

He didn't know what to say. He felt like he was a ship caught in a storm. It was like the demons had hold of him, but now he felt something trying to pull him in a different direction. He felt strength in her words.

She continued, "Daddy, I know there is nothing more powerful than God. Nothing. You taught me that. There is nothing that can hurt us if we have faith in him. I don't know everything you do, and I know you won't tell me everything, but it doesn't matter now. What matters is you and what you are going to do. I want to know if you are going to let these demons continue to do this or if are you going to put a stop to this and take back what belongs to you, especially your country, your family, and your faith in God?"

These words hit him hard. He used to be such a good man. There had been a time when he was proud of the Christian he was. Then, it seemed like he kept making one small mistake, followed by another and then another. He eventually felt he had made too many, and he couldn't find his way back. He hadn't really thought about it like this before. His daughter's words were stirring something in him. She continued to stare at him. Suddenly, he saw his own mother. She had never given up on him, not until the day she died. She had always had faith he would do what was right in the end. He saw that same faith in his daughter now. He was speechless. He didn't know what to say, but she was looking at him like she expected an answer to her question.

He finally asked, "What do you want me to say? What do you want me to do?"

She put a hand on his shoulder and, with surprising softness, said, "Isn't it obvious, Dad? Can't you see? I want you to be the man, the father, and the president I know you can be."

He looked off, deep in thought. It was as if the demons had hold of him and nothing was going to make them let go. He mumbled, "I don't know how to find my way back. It's all just too much."

She strengthened her grip on his shoulder and said, "Then, let me help you."

He shook his head and said, "I don't think you can, baby. I don't know what to do."

She grabbed his face and said, "Do what a Christian man would do. Do what a child of God would do." He stared into her eyes as she said, "Get on your knees and call out for help. That is how you can fight this." As he continued to stare, she reassured him, "You're not alone. You and I can do this together." She pulled him down to his knees.

As they were kneeling on the floor by his desk, she took his trembling hands into her own and prayed, "Lord, I don't know everything my father is battling, but I know you do. My father needs you, Lord. He needs you to intervene. I know you are bigger than the problems he is facing. I know you can overcome anything. Please help my dad, Lord. Please intervene."

She paused, as if she was looking for words or waiting on him to speak. Then, she said, "My father is battling demons, Lord. They are all around him. They are attacking him. Send him an angel, Lord."

And there it was. It was suddenly so clear to him now. Everything made sense. As the realization dawned on him, he began to breathe short, rapid breaths. She stopped praying, opened her eyes, and he continued breathing those short, rapid breaths. Suddenly, he collapsed on her and started sobbing uncontrollably. She held him in her arms as he buried his head into her shoulder and continued to cry. She wasn't sure what was going on. She had never seen her dad act like this, so she asked, "What is it, Dad? What's wrong?"

Through his sobs, he replied, "He already did, baby. He already did."

Chapter Twenty-One

Outskirts of Jerusalem, Israel

Cain stood confidently, watching men, women, and equipment being unloaded in the desert outside the city. A soldier came sprinting up to him, and in the distance behind the soldier, Cain could see three men being marched up slowly. The soldier said, "Sir, our advance units are returning, and we are ready to move into the city."

Cain replied, "No, not yet. I want all our people on the ground and ready. That city must be leveled to the ground. The army has marched out to the west, but there are still people in there that will oppose us. When we move in, I want all our forces concentrated to destroy and kill everyone and everything."

As he finished, the soldier turned and motioned to the men slowly coming up to their position. He said, "Sir, these three priests were on their way into the city. We intercepted them."

Cain, giving the man a glare, said, "And why aren't they already dead?"

The soldier responded, "We tried, sir. Our men fired at them several times, but we couldn't hit them."

Cain continued his glare and said, "Are your men that poor with their weapons?"

The soldier, nervous now, said, "No, um, I mean, the bullets wouldn't hit them."

Cain considered this. He knew about the prophecy of the three priests that would stand in Jerusalem. He knew the Bible. He knew they had a part to play, but his people never believed in the Bible's accuracy. They knew it represented a possibility, but not the one they subscribed to.

Maybe they could not be harmed by mortal men, but he was not merely a man. He was something more, he was Satan's lieutenant, and he would show them his power. He pushed the man aside and, with lightning speed, pulled his blade and beheaded the priest on the left. His body crumpled to the ground. He turned, looked at the soldier, and said, "Don't let old stories intimidate or scare you."

He turned and beheaded the second priest, who was standing defiantly before him. He turned again and said, "You can't believe everything you read in the Bible. It's only one version of what could happen. We make our own future, and this is our time. Nothing can stop us. They will all die before us."

The soldier nodded vigorously. Cain turned to the final priest and drew back his blade, but then, he hesitated. The priest had a look of defiance that he had come to expect from true believers of God. The final priest said, "No matter what you do, you cannot defeat the one and only God."

A smile appeared across Cain's face, and suddenly he changed his mind. He put his blade away and then moved to confront the man. Cain said, "So you are ready to die for your faith?"

The man just looked at Cain.

Inside, Cain was impressed he was so strong. Few had ever stood up to him this way. Cain knew this man would die without hesitation and would do it willingly, freely. Cain said, "You and all like you will now be wiped from the face of the Earth."

The priest spoke in a soft, confident voice, "I know the story, and it sounds as if you do also. It will not end with my death, and you have to know you will not win."

Cain replied, "I have something else in mind for you." Cain walked behind the man and forced him to his knees. Cain said, "Stay there. I will kill you, but first I want you to watch as we wipe out everything you hold dear. I am going to show you how pathetically weak your people and your God are."

Chapter Twenty-Two

✝EL AVIV, ISRAEL

They had been walking for hours, but they knew they were getting close. Job asked the Apostle, "How much farther?"

The Apostle replied, "Not far. We should be near the outskirts when we get just over that rise."

The walk had been quiet. Job felt he had to ask, "What do you think about all of it?"

The Apostle shook his head slowly, "I think we have to have faith, faith that whatever happens, that it is God's will."

Job looked back for a moment at the sea of people walking behind him. He turned back to the Apostle and asked, "What if we all die? Have you thought about that? What if all we have ever been doing is getting ready to end? Who will protect the faithful?"

The Apostle didn't reply, only gave a solemn look.

Then, Job said, "I'm not afraid to die, to lose some of us, but I'm not prepared to lose all of us."

The Apostle put his hand on Job's shoulder and smiled. He said, "The same person that has always protected the faithful always will. Our Lord and Savior. I think whatever happens will be his will. We have to put our faith in God and trust his plans for us all."

Job nodded solemnly.

Trying to lighten the subject, the Apostle said, "As soon as we top this rise, we should be able to see Jerusalem in the distance."

A few moments later, the two men topped the rise. Instantly, they were speechless. The Apostle's arm shot up, and the sea of men and women came to a stop. A few that were close by could see it, and a couple of them gasped audibly. The Apostle's mouth came open, and shock washed over Job. The sight was something they were not prepared for. They were not marching to meet merely armed soldiers. They were marching into the teeth of an army that was organized into neat rows and well equipped.

As the Apostle took it in, he had to look over a great distance to see it all. Large guns, small tanks, and even helicopters hovered in the distance. The road to Jerusalem was cut off, and these people stood between them and the Holy City. For a moment, neither could speak. Then, slowly the Apostle looked at Job, whose eyes were welling up. The Apostle said, "You know we can't turn back. We have to march into that."

Job slowly nodded as more tears fell. He looked back at the mass of people, and all he could think was "lambs to the slaughter." He turned his gaze back to the Apostle and said in a hushed voice, "We are all going to die."

The Apostle returned his gaze and again put a firm hand on his shoulder as he said, "Then, let's die together, brother, for the glory of God."

Job considered his words. He had known this man for many years. Job thought about the options and realized the Apostle was right. There was no other choice. All his life, Job had put his faith in this man and, more importantly, in God. Job looked into the Apostle's eyes and saw the determination. Job reminded himself there was a reason they followed this man, a reason the Apostle was their leader. Feeling inspired, Job returned his gesture. Placing his hand back on the Apostle's shoulder, he said, "Yes, let's do it together, brother."

Chapter Twenty-Three

JORDAN

Eve asked the pilot, "How much longer?"

The pilot screamed, "Ten minutes!"

Eve and her team started to prep their gear. One of the soldiers with her asked, "Ma'am, I couldn't help but think, why here? What is the significance?"

Eve looked at the young woman for a moment. She really didn't know any of these soldiers very well. Everything had happened so fast, she hadn't really had time to do much, besides explain the importance of the mission. In truth, she may not have chosen many of them, but in the chaos, she had to grab who she could and make the best of it. Eve took in the young woman before her, her long black hair, pulled back tightly, round face, and soft, green eyes. Eve asked, "What's your name?"

The young woman replied, "Ellen."

Eve was shocked. Incredulous, she asked, "You haven't chosen a Biblical name? Have you even taken the anointing?"

Ellen replied, "I have, but I have struggled with a name."

Eve asked, "How long have you been with us?"

"Just a few months," Ellen replied.

Eve shook her head. She couldn't believe she had taken someone so green on such a critical mission. Ellen quietly watched as Eve gave her a concerned look. Then, Ellen, sensing her concern, said, "I promise, I won't let you down."

Eve didn't reply. She looked away as she spoke, "Revelation 12-6, the woman and the dragon. She flees into the wilderness. Many believe that place in the wilderness is Petra."

Ellen looked at her with a puzzled look.

Eve simplified her response and repeated, "The answer to your question is Petra. The significance is that it is a holy place for them, and there is nowhere else they would want to go to anoint the child. The Bible tells us people will flee and come here in the tribulation. They read the same Bible we do. They believe people will come here to die at the orders of the Anti-Christ."

Ellen, now looking off herself, continued, "After Armageddon."

Eve looked in her direction but didn't respond. She turned and looked blankly into the distant horizon and said, "There is nowhere else on Earth they would want to take him. They consider this place as holy as we do. Amazing when you think about it. Man has scattered across the globe and explored every inch of this planet, but in the end, it all ends up back here, where it all started, just like he told us it would."

Just as Eve finished talking, the pilot screamed, "Time!"

Eve and her team picked up their gear as the massive helicopter hovered over a canal. While maneuvering the helicopter, the pilot said, "This is as low as I can get you!"

Eve nodded, acknowledging the pilot's statement. After several ropes were dropped out of the helicopter, she and the other soldiers began to drop down the fifty feet to the canal below. Eve knew the geography. Petra was a city carved out of rock, and this canal was water from a dam that was on the other side of the mountain. The entrance was what looked like a city, carved into the side of solid stone. This city was well over two-thousand years old and had actually become a tourist destination. She was sure they wouldn't see any today. With everything going on, no one was coming out, and everyone who lived there was staying indoors.

She had selected the canal bed because it was the least likely route where someone would look for them. Christians believed one of the many tombs here contained the remains of Aaron, Moses's brother. She wasn't totally sure why the Satanists held this place in such high regard, but it was a well-known and accepted fact that both sides believed the place had a special significance. Eve looked ahead at the narrow canyon they were going to walk through and remembered this place had been called "The Lost City." It was, somewhat, ironic, and she said a prayer, asking that they would be able to find the lost child in the caves they would be entering soon.

Eve took the lead in the ankle-deep water. She began splashing to the nearby shore. As the others fell in behind her, she said, "It's about a mile to the entrance."

They silently fell into a line behind her as she moved beside the narrow creek and toward what appeared to be massive rock formations in the distance. She wondered how many Satanists they would face. She and her team were well equipped with lots of ammunition. They were wearing bulletproof vests to protect themselves from the shots they knew they would take. They had sidearms, machine guns, and a combination of back-up weapons. She had never been this heavily armed in her life, and all she could think was, Will it be enough?

Chapter Twenty-Four

ᴜᴜASHINGᴛon, D.C.

The President sat in his office with Jackie and Vice-President Calebs. It was easy to see that he was now a different man. Both Jackie and Calebs had noted the change in him. He was full of energy and had a twinkle in his eye that had been missing for a long time. The President looked at each of them and asked, "Any questions?"

Jackie was stunned, and Calebs stared straight ahead. Neither spoke for a moment. Then, Jackie cleared her throat and said, "Mr. President, are you sure about this?"

The President nodded. He hadn't slept at all the night before, but he couldn't remember the last time he'd felt this good. He and his daughter had stayed up together until the sun came up, talking and praying. After, he had taken a shower and had gotten dressed and had been in meetings all morning. He was taking no chances, and he was talking with only the people he trusted the most.

Vice-President Calebs said, "Mr. President, I will do my part, but honestly, sir, my part is easy compared to yours. You are taking some enormous risks, and I have to ask, 'Are you sure there is no other way?'"

The President smiled, nodded, and replied, "Yes, I am one-hundred-percent sure."

Calebs observed, "Sir, I don't see how you can be so happy about this. This is going to cost you everything."

The President gave him an earnest look and replied, "No, not everything. What I was doing before was going to cost me my soul. Besides, we still have a lot of work to do together. This is a good plan, but everything has to happen on schedule."

They nodded, got up, and left the room. As the rest of them left, an aide entered and gave the President a nervous look. The President motioned for her to approach him as he asked, "What did you find out?"

The aide gave him another nervous glance and replied, "I'm sorry, sir. It's my fault. I, I must have made some type of mistake. Can you give me the name again?"

The President replied, "The name was Wood. Bethany Wood."

The aide continued to look at him while nervously clutching some papers in her hand.

The President said, "It's all right. Go ahead. What is it?"

The aide replied, "I'm sorry, sir. I couldn't find her." She hesitated for a moment. Then, she said, "The only person I could find couldn't possibly be the person you are looking for."

The President replied, "I don't understand."

The aide repeated his instructions, "Bethany Wood from the Christian Coalition."

The President nodded, and the aide continued, "Sir, Bethany Wood is dead."

The President was stunned. He repeated, "Dead. Someone killed her?"

The aide replied, "No, sir, natural causes, about ten years ago."

The President snatched the papers out of her hand, and as he looked through them, the aide continued to speak, "Bethany Wood was a well-known member of the Christian Coalition. one of its first female leaders. She had been to Washington and had met more than one president."

As she was speaking, the President was looking at photos and articles detailing the woman he had tried to find. He looked at several pictures of an old woman, who resembled who he had been looking for, but then he stopped at a black and white photo of her. The aide noticed the change of expression on his face and said, "Sir, that picture was taken when she was around the age of thirty."

The President stared at the picture. He was speechless for a moment. Then, he asked, "Where was this photo taken?"

"Here," came the response. The President looked at the aide as she said, "In 1937, she was meeting with President Roosevelt."

The President was stunned as he stared at the woman he had just seen a few days before.

The aide continued, "Bethany Wood died in 2009 at the age of 102."

The President looked at the picture intensely for some moments. Then, he whispered to himself, "She was telling me what I had to do. She was telling me how we can win this." Suddenly, he broke out into a broad smile as he handed the photos back to the aide and said, "Thank you. Well done."

As he turned to go back to his desk, the aide, puzzled, asked, "Mr. President, I don't understand. What does this all mean?"

While still smiling, he turned, looked at her, and replied, "It means I was never really alone. Even when I didn't realize it, I was getting the help I needed. It means this isn't over. God is still on our side. Tell my press secretary that I have to address the nation."

Chapter Twenty-Five

OUTSKIRTS OF JERUSALEM, ISRAEL

The Apostle knew time was short. He knew what he was asking of them was near impossible, but he was going to do everything he could to ensure they had every chance they could. He spoke to his fellow soldiers and said, "Spread the word. We will be charging soon. Tell them to fix weapons and be ready."

Instantly, the word was being carried across the thousands of people behind him. It was a crude system, but they were making it work. The Apostle had his fellow Apostolate members close. As he looked at each of them, he thought about the army that had hastily assembled from around the world. Looking at the force in front of him, he realized now it was a Gideon's army. They were hopelessly outnumbered and outgunned, but they were past the point of turning back. As the realization of all this hit him, he knew they would need God now more than ever. He said, "Pray with me."

The men and women fell to their knees and closed their eyes. Across the sea of people, they all did the same, each kneeling in a wave. They knew they couldn't all hear the Apostle's prayer, but it was understood that each would pray their own prayer, and in the end, all knew they were in God's hands.

Hearing the noise of so many people kneeling, the Apostle opened his eyes, before he started to pray. This wasn't what he had intended, but the Apostle smiled and closed his eyes again. He prayed in a low voice, "Lord, we are here. We are ready to sacrifice ourselves for you. As always, we are in your hands." He hesitated. He wasn't sure what else he should say. He wanted to pray for his people to survive this, but he knew definitely that some or all would not. He continued aloud, "Lord, we are here this day for you. We are here, on this day, as your servants to do your bidding. Watch over us, Lord. We pray that you help us in the great battle ahead." He paused, wondered what else to say. Nothing else came to him, so he finished, "Amen."

The Apostolate repeated, "Amen."

Then, across the sea of people, they began to slowly echo, "Amen."

Again, the Apostle smiled, looked at the Apostolate, and said, "He says, 'Where two or more gather together in my name, there shall I be.'"

They all instinctively looked back as the Apostle said, "Make no mistake. He is here with us now."

Back in the heart of the sea of people, one did not come to his feet. David continued to pray as those around him got up and prepared themselves. He was not a leader. He wasn't sure what he was supposed to do. He couldn't stop thinking about his son and what he was going through. He kept telling himself that Eve would deliver him. He kept trying to take his mind off him, but it was very hard.

Joseph watched him continue to pray. He had stayed close to David during the march. He could feel God's presence around David. Joseph knew the end was coming, but he could still feel the potential for the pendulum to swing either way. He could feel the Spirit in the air, but he knew Satan's demons were also on the loose, and he worried for his brothers and sisters. So much seemed to rest on so few, and he worried about that. He needed to hear something,

something to give this meaning, something to give him focus for what lie ahead.

David, aware of Joseph's presence close to him, heard Joseph ask, "Are you hearing anything? Is he speaking to you?"

David, with his eyes still closed, shook his head. "No, nothing yet."

Joseph asked, "Can you tell me anything, anything about what we are marching into?"

David slowly opened his eyes. He noticed the Christian flag standard being carried in the distance. Then, it was given to him. This was going to be close. It was going to be so close. Moments and seconds would decide the outcome, and nothing was certain. In the end, they all still had free will and so much would depend on how they used that free will and when they would use it. David was still staring at the flag, watching it blow in the breeze. He nodded toward it and somberly replied, "Only that if that flag touches the ground, it will never rise again."

Joseph wanted to make a difference. For his entire life, he had believed he would do something special, but he had never been able to realize what. He had always carried his family's disappointment of him. They never understood why he didn't take up the ministry, but he had always believed God wanted him to be with these people. He had always believed there was a reason he was here. As he considered this and everything else that had happened, he looked in the direction of the flag as it blew in the wind, pondering the implications of what he had heard.

Chapter Twenty-Six

PETRA, JORDAN

As the goat's throat was slit, it let out a gurgle. Then, it fell to the ground with involuntary jerks and fits. Blood pooled around its body. Only true Satanists understood the significance of the goat. It was their most sacred animal. As the Chairman dipped the knife in the pool of blood that was already forming, she looked up and took in her surroundings. From behind the stone altar, she looked at the dozens of men and women she had brought with her, all dressed in white. She looked at the stone pillars that lined into the distance behind her men and the high canyon walls that rose up to a very high, natural stone ceiling. Torches had been lit everywhere, and the artificial light from their flames gave the entire area an eerie glow.

The Chairman was dressed in an all-white, flowing gown that went to her feet. She wasn't wearing shoes. As she raised the knife into the air to begin the ceremony, she felt inspired. She knew her master had to be so proud of all she had done in his name, and she felt his spirit all around her now. She said, "Praise him! Praise his name. Hail Lucifer!"

The dozens of men and women around her repeated, "Hail Lucifer! Hail Lucifer!"

The Chairman smiled broadly. This was going to be one of the best nights of her life. She motioned, and Judas, who was carrying the child, began climbing the steps to the altar. She laid the knife down, squatted over the goat, and pushed her hands into the warm blood, soaking both of them in it. She put them to her face. She looked up and loudly said, "As we do this, we have assembled an army in the Middle East. This army will destroy the Christians and the city of Jerusalem!"

Cheers erupted from the soldiers as she continued, "The time is upon us. When this ceremony is complete, we will bring the anointed one our master told us was coming. The same one the Christian Bible predicted was coming in Revelation! We will set him on his throne, and with our master, he will RULE!"

Cheers erupted again. They echoed because of the high ceiling. They were deafening. Eve and her ten men and women were looking down on them. Eve had positioned her soldiers in a high place, and they were staring at them from a good position. Eve estimated they were, at least, one hundred feet above the Satanists, and she had every exit covered. She looked around. Her soldiers looked frightened. She realized they had to be outnumbered by more than six to one. She reminded herself, This is not my elite army. Instead, this was a ragtag group of soldiers she had pulled together at the last minute, and she had to put them at ease. They were waiting on the return of one soldier. He arrived quietly and out of breath. Eve asked, "Did you get them all in place?"

"Yes, just as we discussed," came the reply.

Eve nodded and then looked at each of them for a moment. She said, "I know you are frightened. Remember, fear is natural. You have to control it. That child down there is why we are here. Everything depends on us rescuing him and not letting them complete the ceremony. We have the high ground. We have the element of surprise. We have to make one soldier feel like ten. We have to feel like one hundred soldiers to them. Remember your training." She hoped her words had helped them. It was time for them to strike. They would have to move quickly, and she knew they only had a few minutes to begin the attack. She knew what would happen if they failed. She looked at each of them for a moment, taking time to look them each in the eye. Then, she said, "Let us pray."

Chapter Twenty-Seven

ШASHINGፐON, D.C.

The President entered the outside area of the House chamber. He had requested this quickly, and Congress had been hastily assembled. Vice-President Calebs was waiting on him. As the President approached, they exchanged a warm handshake. The vice-president leaned in and said, "Is there anything I can do, Mr. President?"

The President smiled and shook his head as he said, "No. Just be ready. Be ready when you are needed. I will start it, but it will be up to you to finish it."

Calebs nodded solemnly and said, "I will see you inside, sir."

The President turned to Bays and asked, "Are you sure you are up to this?"

Bays replied, "Yes, sir. I'm with you."

The President put a hand on his shoulder and said, "What we do next may end your career."

Bays replied, "I am with you till the end. I've been thinking of a new career anyway." Bays smiled and said, "I'm pretty flexible. I can find another line of work. There's always retail management."

The President let himself enjoy a slight chuckle. Then, he replied, "You? In a store full of people? Yeah, I would like to see that someday." He suddenly changed expressions and, with a serious look, said, "Let's go."

Bays pulled his wrist to his mouth and said, "We are moving."

As they approached the door, they could hear someone say, "Mr. Speaker, the president of the United States!"

As they burst through the doors, Congress applauded, and the President slowly moved down the aisle, stopping to shake hands with various people as he went. For a few minutes, he was a politician again, giving firm handshakes and that winning smile he was so well-known for.

As he approached the end, Young was waiting patiently for his handshake, with a big, broad, disarming smile on his face. The President knew he had to shake his hand, and to Young's surprise, the President gave him a firm handshake with both hands and a surprisingly warm smile.

Young, stunned for a second, quickly recovered and pulled him close. With his trademark smile, he whispered something in the President's ear that only he could hear, "You didn't clear this with us. Not sure what you are doing, but you need to remember your daughter. Her very life depends on her father putting her first."

The President pulled away, still smiling broadly, aware of the eyes and cameras on them both. With Young's hand in his grip, he pulled him back toward him and placed his left hand on Young's arm as he replied, "Don't worry, Morris. I know exactly what comes first in my life."

He pulled away and began to climb the steps to the podium. He shook hands with Speaker Harris and Vice-President Calebs. He turned and heard more scattered applause.

As the applause died down, he grabbed both sides of the podium, bowed his head, and silently said a prayer to himself, "I'm here, Lord. I'm ready. Please give me the strength and the words." After taking a deep breath, he began, "My fellow Americans…"

Chapter Twenty-Eight

OUTSKIRTS OF JERUSALEM, ISRAEL

The fighting was everywhere, hand to hand, guns blazing, both at a distance and at point-blank range. People on both sides were falling by the dozens. Overall, the battle was going against the Christians, who were being steadily pushed back by the superior firepower and air support. But they kept coming and coming. They would not quit.

In the midst of the battle, David knew this was it. It was his time. They had staked everything on this. Screams, gunshots, and explosions were all around him, but he couldn't hear any of it. He knew now was the moment when he had to run. He came running through the middle of the Christian lines. Seemingly out of nowhere, he emerged and began to swing his blade violently. He was hitting no one and taking out enemy soldiers with every wave of his sword. With every swing of his arm, the energy came from him and dozens of soldiers fell dead. David kept running until he was far ahead of his people.

In the distance, Cain received a report from a man who had run without stopping to deliver this message to him. With his chest heaving, he put his hands on his knees to catch his breath. After taking in a gulp of air, he reported, "The situation on our right is desperate! We are trying to pull the people out, but we can't stop him!"

Cain thought for a moment. He had placed all the imps in front. His soldiers were in tight layers, closer to his own position, so he wasn't immediately concerned. He quietly congratulated himself on his strategic thinking. He looked at his panicked subordinate who was still breathing hard, and he asked, "How many do you estimate they have there?"

The man gulped air again and replied, "We are in full retreat on the right. We are trying to get them out, but we can't stop him."

Cain stared at him for a moment. Then, he asked, "He? Are you saying our entire right flank is in full retreat from one man?"

The man gulped air again and replied, "He's killing them all!"

Cain knew now who he meant. Again, he remembered his planning. He was ready for David. He could waste his power on his cannon fodder if he wanted. They mattered little to him. Cain raised a radio clipped to his belt and said, "Patience. Let him get closer."

Across the field, David was running with everything inside of him. The Christians were still being pushed back in the center and the left, but on the right, David was making a huge dent in their line.

Far behind the front, Joseph stopped and pulled his binoculars. He could see David moving forward, all alone. The sight was like nothing he could have imagined. Hundreds, maybe thousands of people were shooting at David but, somehow, not hitting him. Behind Joseph, he heard one of the soldiers say, "It's a suicide run. It's only a matter of time before they get him."

Joseph didn't respond. He just continued to watch. David ran up a small rise covered with troops. He waved his arm, and energy came from his body, throwing the men and women in all directions. David ran over the rise and down the other side.

Out of breath, he stopped for a moment. He was completely exhausted. No one had followed him, and now he was being surrounded by troops. Suddenly, several tanks appeared, coming from different directions. He couldn't go anymore. He collapsed to his knees and tried to catch his breath. Then, several helicopters began to appear around him. As he gulped in air and looked around, he realized he was surrounded. In the distance, Cain watched through a pair of binoculars. While he did, he heard his radio chirp. He picked it up and said, "Go ahead."

One of the pilots in one of the helicopters surrounding David replied, "Ready, sir."

Cain smiled broadly. He had to pause for a moment to take it all in. He was so fortunate to witness, not only the extermination of the Christian army, but also the extermination of this thorn in his side.

David felt his anger flair. Defiantly, he stood up and straightened himself. His chest was heaving. He looked around at all the guns pointed at him, along with the helicopters and tanks. He wondered if he had been forsaken. Was this the end? Had he played his part? His thoughts went to his son. He hoped, if he survived, somehow, he would understand.

The wind started to pick up and blow hard. The soldiers on both sides had to stop and take notice. The sky darkened, seemingly instantly, and a thick, white mist descended over the entire area, which began to block out the sun. Out of the mist overhead, a smaller stream of mist drifted downward, and out of that mist came a hand, which wrapped its long fingers around David.

Suddenly, David felt the hand closing in on him. He was in its grip, and he could not move. David jerked and twisted, but he couldn't budge. The large hand had totally consumed him. In front of David and across all the soldiers who could see this part of the field, the Satanist soldiers screamed, "Praise Satan! Praise our lord!" The screams echoed across the field and drifted back to the wild cheers breaking out around Cain. He continued smiling and said to those around him with pride, "He is interceding directly now!"

As thunder roared and lightning struck around the field, a storm descended on the battle. The wind and lightning seemed to be everywhere now. Various items, too numerous to count, blew across the men and women in the vast wind that hit them all.

Cain looked around and screamed to those close to him, "Do you see?! Do you see?! This is power! This is our god!"

The radio chirped again, and Cain heard someone report, "All Christian soldiers are in full retreat across our front."

Cheers erupted as Cain suddenly remembered the pilot waiting for an order. Cain pulled the radio to his mouth and simply said, "Kill him."

The pilot knew the plan. They were all ready for his signal, and with this first shot, they were to all fire in unison. He wanted to just pull the trigger, but the sight of Satan intervening in the battle had inspired him, so he screamed into his headpiece, "In the name of Lucifer, fire!"

Guns erupted in near-perfect unison and poured fire into the pit David was in. The fire was steady and unceasing for several moments. Then, as clips began to go empty, the helicopters shot missiles, and the tanks began lobbing shells onto the position David was in, which could not be seen for the fire and explosions around it.

In the midst of this chaos, David was still inside the tight fist, and nothing was touching him. He felt the Holy Spirit wash over him. At first, it felt wrong and out of place, but it was unmistakable. David knew God was with him. He didn't know what it meant, so he closed his eyes and let God talk to him. He waited to hear a voice, but he didn't. He just felt peace and serenity. As the last of the shells fired, missiles launched and bullets were used, the smoke slowly began to clear. David was still standing in the grip of the hand, unharmed.

In the distance, Joseph couldn't believe it was over. He had held out hope they could turn this around, but without David, he knew it was useless. He was still looking through his binoculars, praying for a miracle. When it was over, he could see David was still standing.

Joseph was being suffocated by the mob of people trying to get away to safety. He slowly began to realize what had happened, and more importantly, he realized he was the only one that had noticed. As the realization dawned on him, he screamed at the mob of retreating soldiers as they ran by him, "Look!"

A few stopped, but most kept running for their lives as explosions boomed around them. More and more of the Christians kept dropping from gunfire and explosions. It was clear they had lost. Now, they had to get out.

Cain, looking from the opposite direction, furious, ordered the remaining tanks to turn from chasing the Christians and to converge on David's position.

David's eyes were still closed. He slowly opened them as the Satanic soldiers stared in disbelief. Thunder and lightning boomed all around. As a clap of thunder exploded, a voice boomed that seemed to come from the sky above: "You have been and shall always be my child. Even when you didn't know you served me, you did."

For some reason, David began to cry. He felt the Spirit surround him, and he knew he was in the presence of the Father, but he didn't feel worthy. He looked off in the distance and saw his brothers and sisters retreating.

The voice boomed again, "My children need a leader. Now go! Lead them!"

David felt his body tingle all over, and he felt totally rejuvenated as the hand holding him vanished with a wisp of wind.

Far in the distance, Joseph jumped up and down as he screamed at the top of his lungs, "It was the hand of God! It was the hand of God!"

For a moment, David just stood there, looking at the people around him. Then, his power welled up inside of him and exploded out of him in every direction, killing the soldiers and destroying the tanks and helicopters around him. Another flood of Satanist soldiers had been ordered to converge on him, and with his blade still in his hands, he chased after them, bursts of energy taking out dozens with each swing of his arm.

In the distance, Joseph screamed, "He's not dead! He's not dead!" He had the attention of a few around him, but most were still not listening.

Joseph waded into the flood of retreating people, elbowing and pushing his way forward through the mob while screaming, "We have to push forward!" Even though, the mass of people pushing by him seemed like they would crush him, he continued pushing, seemingly in the wrong direction, but he knew had to do something. They had a small chance if only they could see.

When he spotted a soldier carrying their flag, Joseph ran up to the retreating soldier and jerked it away from him. Joseph, then, ran up a small rise and raised the flag as high as he could.

In the dusk that had settled on the battlefield, the wind caught the large flag which spread out in full, and Joseph began to swing it from right to left with all his might. He felt like even the wind was against him. It strained him to his limits to keep the flag up. No one was looking, but he kept swinging it as hard as he could. When his arms began to ache from the motion, he continued. He refused to quit. As his strength waned and desperation filled him, he screamed with all his might, "IN THE NAME OF JESUS!"

As this echoed across the battlefield, a bullet pierced his body, then another, and another. Joseph fell to his knees, shock and dizziness overtaking him, as he saw the last of the Christian soldiers retreating past him. Slowly, he began falling, face first, directly toward the ground, but he stopped himself with his left arm as his kness hit the ground hard. With blood pouring from several wounds, he pushed the flag back into the air with his right arm and waved it feebly. Defiantly, he pushed the flag upward, not giving up until the last moments of his life. He had given it his best try, but in the end, it just wasn't enough.

As the flag was falling with him, just a moment before the last of his strength gave way, it was snatched away by a soldier who was inspired to rush forward and grab it, inches before it touched the ground. Suddenly, a few soldiers spontaneously turned around and surged forward again, past Joseph.

In his last moments, lying there on the ground with the life ebbing out of him, he was able to see the tide turn and see that his brothers and sisters were, once again, on the attack. A slight smile crossed his lips. Then, he heard a voice say, "Well done, my good and faithful servant. Now come on home."

Joseph never stopped smiling.

Chapter Twenty-Nine

PETRA, JORDAN

Everyone was in position. Eve took a long look around and made one last check. She put her wrist to her mouth and said, "It's time. Set the timer." With this, she picked up her rifle and began sprinting across the top of the stone path that overlooked the Satanists. They had made the mistake of thinking they were here in secret, and Eve felt they had the element of surprise.

As she stopped, she took a knee and quickly put the rifle scope to her eye. Through the scope, the child was visible, and he was lying on a stone altar. The Chairman was slowly wiping the goat's blood on him with her bare hands. Eve had the Chairman's head in her crosshairs. She slowly squeezed her trigger as the bombs went off in unison. The vibration from the explosions shook the entire area. As a result, the shot that should have killed the Chairman missed her.

The explosion was deafening. Every exit, except one, was now sealed off. The Satanists were quick to respond, the ceremony stopped as Judas pushed forward, through the ensuing chaos, to protect the Chairman. He pushed himself between her and the infant as she commanded, "Take him!"

The baby was screaming as Judas picked him up and bullets whizzed all around. Judas and the Chairman began to run toward the back of the large stone room, down a long stone hallway.

Eve had positioned her people well, and they were raining fire down on the Satanists. However, the Satanists were all armed, and they had recovered from the initial shock of the explosion and were now returning fire. One of Eve's soldiers took a bullet in the neck and fell to his death. The other soldiers continued their fire as Eve watched the Chairman and Judas flee. She screamed into her wrist, "They're on the run! I need backup! I'm going after them!"

Ellen was nearby. She had just emptied her clip. She ejected it and slammed another into her rifle. She put her wrist to her mouth and said, "I'm coming!" She jogged off as the remaining soldiers continued the firefight.

Eve sprinted to the far end of the arena. She spotted the opening they had run through moments before. She looked for a way down but could not find one. She was frantic now. She had to hurry.

Out of desperation, she looked at the jagged rock formations that made up the walls. When she spotted an area she thought she could use, she took a deep breath. Then, she ran and jumped. She felt herself fall. Somehow, she managed to catch herself on a nearby piece of rock.

While hanging on to that rock, she looked for another. When she found it, she jumped down again. This continued until she was about halfway down. At this point, she had gotten to a place where there were no more rocks for her to grab. She looked around and spotted one to her right, but it was far away. She knew the jump would be difficult, and she could feel her hands slipping.

She pulled herself back. Then with everything inside her, she pushed with her legs and pulled with her arms. She exploded across the rocks. Her left foot landed safely on the rock she was aiming for.

She grabbed hold of the wall as best she could, while gasping for air. She needed a moment to catch her breath, but suddenly, her foot gave way, and she fell. She felt her body hitting the rock wall as she tumbled. She grabbed for whatever she could and managed to grab a rock. This stopped her fall. Now she was only about ten feet from the ground.

After taking a deep breath, she let herself go. She hit the ground and rolled until she came to a stop. Her ribs ached as she came to her feet. She pulled her rifle but realized the barrel had been damaged during the fall. She threw it to the ground and took off running. Ellen saw her running into the stone hallway far below. She realized she would have to go down the same way. She took a long breath. Then, she made her first jump.

Chapter Thirty

WASHINGTON, D.C.

The speech had been going on for some time. The President had been outlining the conflicting points of view, regarding the Middle East, the countries involved, and the number of soldiers currently amassed for an invasion at the Israeli border. These were all facts everyone knew, and it was beginning to sound like just another long, boring political speech. The President glanced down at Young, who had been staring intently at first, but he saw that Young was now looking more at ease and almost sleepy. The President paused. Then, he took in a long breath and a look around. The silence seemed to get everyone's attention. After clearing his throat, he said, "Now that we have outlined everything that is going on, let's look at our own country. As you know, we have done nothing and have claimed neutrality in the coming conflict. I would like to tell you this was my plan and my administration's goal, but that would be a lie."

Suddenly, rumblings could be heard, and everyone in the chamber began talking.

The President spoke again, "My friends, know this. There are traitors among us."

The talking quieted, and everyone was now looking intently at the President as he continued, "There has been an attempted coup, a coup, not only to usurp my presidency, but to usurp our entire democracy. I have recently been made aware of a movement within our government to attempt to subvert our democratic institutions. Unfortunately, this has been going on for a long time."

Several congressmen and senators seated behind Young began to get up and scream at the President. When Young looked back at them and gave them a stern look, they sat back down. Young glared at the President as he continued, "I, myself, am not free from blame. The minute I knew something of this magnitude was going on, I should have come down here and pointed a finger in your direction." He pointed with his forefinger and moved it across the chamber. He paused. Then, he pointed it directly at Young and said, "I should have pointed a finger in your direction and called you what you are — a traitor!"

Young quickly got up to leave, but as he turned to go up the aisle, he was confronted by Bays. Young said, "Move out of my way, boy."

Bays smiled and said, "I don't think so. You need to sit back down."

Young attempted to push by him, but Bays shoved him back toward his chair, and Young nearly fell. Somewhat embarrassed, with all eyes on him, he moved back to confront Bays who was still blocking his way. Young pushed his face to within a few inches of Bays and said, "You have no idea what you are doing or whom you are dealing with."

Bays, still smiling, motioned with his right arm for Young to take his seat, but Young refused. Then, he tried to push by Bays a second time. Bays grabbed the large man with an ease and speed that shocked Young. Bays spun Young around, and suddenly Young could feel his left arm being pushed behind his back. Bays said, "You're finished."

Young scowled as he twisted his head around in an effort to look at Bays, as he replied, "You have no idea what you've done. You have no idea how powerful I am."

Bays pulled him around with what felt like an iron grip on his left arm, still pushed behind his back. Shock washed over the room, and gasps could be heard. Most were staring with gaping mouths, in complete shock. Bays put his mouth near Young's ear and said, "Walk." Bays began to walk Young up the long aisle, in plain view of all of Congress and the world.

Young, still scowling, twisted his head again and said, "You think I'm alone? You think I don't have colleagues, many colleagues? You would need an army to take us all."

Bays, a thin smile on his face, replied, "Yeah, I think we have that covered."

At that moment, the doors sprang open, and armed soldiers marched into the chamber. Congressman and senators, still in shock, exchanged frightened glances, as the troops continued to file in and encircle the members of Congress. Bays continued to walk Young out of the chamber as he screamed at the top of his lungs, "You can't do this! I am a United States senator!"

As Bays and Young exited the chamber, the President spoke again, "We know these traitors have a mark, a mark that signifies their faith and allegiance. Their allegiance to something other than our government. Ladies and gentlemen, I am invoking Article 83 under the Homeland Security Act. For those of you who may not fully understand, Article 83 allows me to conduct any investigation, with powers used at my discretion, if I believe our government is threatened." He let that sink in for a moment.

As he paused, he reflected on the arrogance of these people. They had become so powerful. They had made only a modest attempt to conceal their mark. He had wondered if this mark could even be the beginnings of the mark of the beast, foretold in the Bible. He had seen Young's because Young was so proud of it and had made a point to show it to him more than once. Now he would use their arrogance, their absolute confidence in their power, against them. He continued, "Now, I need to ask each of you to remove any watches you may be wearing. Soldiers will be coming around and will need to see your wrists."

Chapter Thirty-One

OUTSKIRTS OF JERUSALEM, ISRAEL

A t first, it was just a few dozen, but slowly, more and more Christians began to stop retreating and turn around. The attacking Satanists had broken out in applause and celebration. Many Satanist soldiers were out of bullets or had simply stopped chasing the Christians and laid their guns down altogether. Suddenly, a mass of Christian soldiers began to overrun them, many of the Satanists never saw them coming. Once it was clear the tide of the battle had turned, some Satanists began to pick up their weapons again, but most were either killed or began to run.

At the forefront of the Christian counterattack, a group of Christians overran a tank and, after killing the crew, who had gotten out to celebrate, took it. One Christian jumped on top and said, "Turn the turret around!"

The turret let out a groan as it turned, and he screamed, "Fire!"

The fire from the tank began pouring out across the retreating Satanists and wiping large holes in the lines of their retreating soldiers. As this was happening, David was moving across the field, wiping large holes in the lines himself. With every movement of his hand, he would take out dozens and dozens of soldiers. As the Christians advanced to within sight of him, they cheered and continued to push forward, despite many falling as they did. Cain, furious, screamed into his radio, "I want him dead! Now!"

No one replied.

David kept advancing through the mob of people.

Someone ran up to Cain and said, "Sir! The Christians just broke through our right, and they are compromising us on the left! The center is about to cave in! We have to retreat!"

Cain replied, "That's impossible!"

The man looked at him awkwardly and nodded, not knowing what else to say.

Cain pointed to the battle and said, "I want you to go and have that man killed. Now!"

Scared, the man nodded and ran away. Fuming, Cain watched as David moved closer and closer to his own position. The last priest on his knees in front of Cain smiled as he said, "You can't stop him. The hand of God is on him." As he finished this statement, he looked down to see Cain's blade protruding from his midsection.

Cain leaned down and whispered into the priest's ear, "Your God didn't stop me from taking your life, and he will not stop me from taking his."

Then, he pulled the blade out with a quick motion and kicked the priest to the ground. He fell, face first. Cain realized the priest had been right about one thing — they wouldn't be able to stop him. He would have to do it. He glanced around and saw some dunes in the distance. He nodded to himself as he realized that was where the final battle would have to take place. David spotted Cain in the distance. He began to run in that direction. He saw Cain kick a man to the ground, then take off jogging. David knew he had to go after him. He looked around, and with another wave of his arm, he took out the last helicopter, which spun in a circle, before crashing and exploding on the ground, taking several more Satanist soldiers with it.

What was happening on the battlefield was nothing short of miraculous. David had to stop for a moment and just take it in. The poorly trained Gideon's army had taken on a much larger, more superiorly equipped force and was beating them. He allowed a smile to come across his face. Then, far across the field, he saw Job. His face was dirty and ashen, but he was out in front, leading the advance. For a moment, their eyes met. David nodded and Job returned the nod. David knew he understood, as he turned and ran after Cain. Job continued to look in his direction as he murmured, "God speed, David. God speed."

As the women and men continued to surge forward, a soldier watching the exchange asked, "Where's he going?"

Job turned and said, "He is about his father's business." He put a hand on the man's shoulder and said, "Now we should be also. Too many good people have died for us to stop now. We must keep pushing forward."

David glanced over his shoulder as the battle moved further and further into the distance behind him. He moved into the dense field of dunes and took a deep breath, knowing what was coming. It was destiny. He could see it now. They were always going to end up here. David began to run forward, deeper and deeper into a thick darkness that settled as he moved deeper into the dunes. Then, he saw Cain, standing shirtless, waiting for him calmly. Cain had his serrated blade pulled, at his side, still red with blood dripping from the end.

David's blade was, also, at his side, in his right hand. The two closed in on each other. Slowly, they circled one another. David saw the red glow of Cain's eyes. As they continued to close in on each other, the ground let out a soft tremble, making it seem as though these two powers, being this close, were straining the very ground beneath them. The darkness seemed to grow, and the redness of Cain seemed to become more prominent. David, then, realized his own body was giving off a soft glow.

Cain said, "It was always going to be here. It was always going to be us."

David nodded. It was eerie, but the inevitability was not lost on him. Both were seeing this battle now. Both were being shown this would be the end for one of them. David took in Cain's red body, the glow of the tattoos that covered him, the bulging veins in his arms, and the musculature across his torso. David knew none of that mattered. This battle was spiritual. Their physical bodies would not win this.

Cain spoke again, "I have had so many opportunities to kill you, so many chances to end your life. Now, you will get no more chances. You have chosen your side, and now you will die with it!" He lunged forward with a massive swing of his blade.

David deflected it and moved to the side as Cain went by him. Cain quickly turned and lunged again. This time, David stood his ground and began parrying his swings. The speed of the swings was astonishing. Both men were swinging, dodging, and deflecting at an amazing rate. David was going toe to toe with Cain, and neither man was backing down. Cain screamed and swung downward. David parried. Then, he delivered a knee to Cain's midsection. Cain staggered backward as David moved in to capitalize. David came in with an overhead swing of his own, but Cain swung hard from a side angle and deflected the blow.

The movement staggered both men. The ferocity of the swings caused both men's blades to go sailing through the air. Cain punched David in the nose, and blood poured as David's eyes began to water. David delivered a feeble kick, but it was enough to keep Cain off him. Both men staggered in different directions to pick up their blades. As each recovered their weapons, they stood and looked at each other with their chests heaving.

Cain looked up and saw dark images circling above him. David's eyes instinctively followed Cain's. The dark, shadowy figures with red eyes were circling over Cain's head. One stopped, stared at David, and gave a hissing sound. It was unlike anything David had ever heard before. This inspired Cain, and he again surged forward, swinging wildly. David felt his body tingle. He raised his left hand, and Cain flew backward through the air. He landed on his back with a hard thud. His blade skidded across the ground, stopping a few feet away. David lunged forward after Cain and tried to drive his blade into Cain with a stabbing motion, but he felt it stop mid-air. Stunned, he looked into Cain's eyes, which were also wide. Slowly, the demons materialized. They were all around him. They were holding David back, and Cain's expression quickly changed into a wide grin as he rolled and picked his blade up off the ground. David's arms were frozen, and he couldn't move them. He was grunting and straining, but the demons flying overhead were circling in a tight formation over his head, and Cain understood. Cain couldn't resist. He smiled broadly as he said, "Did you really think my master wouldn't release every demon in Hell to support me?! Did you really think this would be a fair fight?!" Cain slowly pulled his blade over his head and simply said, "This is long overdue."

Chapter Thirty-Two

PETRA, JORDAN

Eve couldn't wait for backup. She exploded down the stone hallway. Even though the hallway was very dark, she ran at top speed as she approached a large opening. As she entered the open area, she stopped and took in her surroundings. In the dimly lit area, she looked at a very high ceiling. The floor in the makeshift room was filled with scattered, chest-high rocks everywhere. Eve pulled her sidearm and pointed it around. Across the vast space, she could barely make out Judas as he moved through an opening on the opposite side. He was carrying the child who was still screaming.

Eve began to run again, as hard as she could. Then, without warning, she felt her chest hit the ground hard. Her gun went spinning off into the darkness. The Chairman had tripped her. Now Eve lay there, breathless, certain she had, at least, one broken rib now. She pushed herself up with her arms in an attempt to get back to her feet, but she had no strength, so she fell back onto her chest. She rolled, and in the dim light, she saw the Chairman in her all-white outfit as she pulled a long sword from a scabbard she was holding in her right hand. The Chairman tossed the scabbard aside and swung downward. Eve rolled, but the long blade caught her shoulder and made a deep cut. She felt her adrenaline kick in, and she managed to get to her feet and duck behind a rock as another swing narrowly missed her head and made sparks fly as it glanced off the rock. Eve turned, and for the first time, the two made eye contact. Eve could see the hate in the Chairman's eyes. This gave her a moment of rest.

The two stared at each other as Eve's chest heaved, and she struggled to catch her breath. The Chairman fainted to her left. Then, she quickly exploded to her right. Eve knew she didn't have the speed to keep up with this woman. Instead of trying to dodge her blow, Eve lunged at her and managed to get a hand on her left hand, her sword hand. Eve's left hand locked on the Chairman's right forearm, and the two grunted against each other, each trying to gain an advantage. Eve, still trying to recover, sucked in a deep breath of air. Then, she dropped to her knees. In a fast movement, she pulled the Chairman on top of her. Then, with her powerful legs, she was able to flip her over her head. The Chairman hit the stone floor with a loud thud. The movement had drained Eve, and both women now staggered to their feet and started to circle each other.

Amazingly, the Chairman still held on to her long, ceremonial sword, and she held it loosely in her left hand. Eve reached into a pocket on her right thigh and pulled out a large knife with her right hand. She held it and moved behind one of the large stones. The two women began to attempt attacks. The Chairman swung the long sword with impressive speed, as Eve ducked behind a rock formation. Eve attempted a stabbing motion with her knife, which the Chairman easily dodged.

As the two circled each other, the Chairman found her moment in the fight and made a hard swing, which Eve dodged, but it caused her to stagger back. The Chairman was unable to capitalize. Her sword had become lodged in the jagged rock from the ferocity of the swing. Eve recovered and lunged forward with her knife. The Chairman was still trying to pull the sword from the rock but saw the move coming and moved to the side. Eve was able to cut her right arm, but the Chairman delivered a hard punch to Eve's nose, which she instantly knew was broken as blood began to pour out of it.

As her eyes watered, she felt a hard kick to the back of her head, and she hit the ground face-first. Eve saw stars and tried to think through the pain of her nose and the deep scratches on her face. She rolled to her back and tried to blink away the tears.

The Chairman grunted and pulled the sword from the rock formation. Eve was drained, and she knew she was at the end. In that moment, she knew she had nothing left physically, so she called on God. Eve screamed out, "Please, God, help me!"

The Chairman couldn't resist. A thin smile crossed her lips as she drew the sword back over her head and said, "This is how your god helps you."

For some reason, Eve was not afraid. She had fought so hard, for so long. She was both mentally and physically exhausted. As the sword came down, Eve closed her eyes and prepared herself to go into eternity.

Chapter Thirty-Three

WASHINGTON, D.C.

The scene was surreal. For the first time in history, armed soldiers were lining the great halls. The President had stood at the podium, watching as the members of Congress were forcibly searched. Anyone bearing the circular mark was arrested and removed. As the last one, a female representative, was identified, she defiantly turned to the President and screamed, "Traitor!"

The President didn't respond. As the soldiers returned to their positions, the President took a deep breath and looked around. The arrests had emptied over half the assembled delegates. The President had allowed this to be filmed by the media, but now the cameras all turned back to him as he began to speak, "I know this is shocking and unprecedented. I know we will spend months, maybe even years, trying to figure out what happened here today. I have a press conference that will be convened at three o'clock this afternoon, where I will try to begin the healing process of our nation. For now, please know we are not a dictatorship. We are not an autocratic country. I am not usurping power. I am exercising the power given to me by the Homeland Security Act, power that could easily be misused. This power was designed to protect us from a domestic threat."

He looked around again and saw a mix of fright and anger. He looked directly into the camera and said, "Today, on my order and on my sole responsibility, our forces are moving into the Middle East. There are forces already engaged there. Our intelligence has already monitored a small engagement outside of Jerusalem. The combined Arab nations have an army of well over a million men gathered along the northeastern border of Israel, and they are being opposed by every man, woman, and child the Israelis can muster. It is our belief this action was precipitated, not by a rival nation, but ultimately, by a faction here in the U.S. It is our belief the entire world has been manipulated, and now we could all pay the price."

The President could see surprise and shock wash over the remaining women and men in the chamber. He took another long breath. Then, he said, "I know not all of you agree, but I want to say to everyone watching that I believe in God. I know this is not a popular belief anymore, but we founded this nation on him. Now, after everything you have just seen and heard, I am going to do something that no president has done in a long time. I want to ask every American … everywhere … to stop what you are doing, if possible, to get on your knees, and to say a prayer for our troops, for Israel, and for the countries opposing Israel. I have come to believe they have all been manipulated. I am asking for everyone in America to take one minute, to get on your knees, and pray that God intercedes directly, that his hand is felt on both sides of this conflict."

The President looked around and saw some disgust, some people shaking their heads in disbelief, but some agreed with him. With the cameras still on him, he stepped to the side of the podium, got on his knees, closed his eyes, and began to pray.

Across America, the spark he lit slowly caught fire. Then, it began to spread, as Americans everywhere followed their president's lead.

❦

In a McDonald's in Virginia, Amera Mullins, watching on a nearby TV, stopped her children from playing as she said, "Kylah, Carter, get over here!"

As the children approached, frustrated that they had to stop playing, she told them to get on their knees with her. As another woman was shaking her head in disgust at the sight, other patrons and employees took notice. Surprisingly, more people joined her, until almost everyone in the dining area was praying. As the disgusted woman looked around, she realized that even the employees had begun to pray. As the drive-through began to back up, with horns honking, the disgusted woman realized she was the only one not praying.

In a garage in Arizona, the owner, who had been watching TV in an office, stuck his head out the door and screamed for his mechanics to come in. As they entered, wiping dirty hands on their grease-stained uniforms and sweat from their foreheads, they saw the TV and that the bottom of the screen read: "President Leads Americans in Prayer."

The owner, said, "Let's go."

With that, he got on his knees, and several followed him. One mechanic looked at them incredulously and said, "Boss, I don't pray. I don't even know how."

The man looked back at him and said, "Then, I'll teach you. If our president can get on his knees on national TV, then we can, too."

The man went to his knees and so did every customer in the waiting room.

At a school in Texas, a high school teacher who had allowed her students to watch the President asked her entire class to pray with her, and most complied. A few doodled or looked at their phones while the others prayed. While this was happening, someone alerted the principal, who burst in, ordering them to stop. The teacher refused, and the principal said, "You know prayer is not allowed in schools. This could mean the end of your career."

The teacher smiled and replied, "Then, consider this my resignation." She closed her eyes and continued.

As the principal looked on in shock, the remaining children, now inspired, got on their knees and joined the teacher.

In Orlando, Florida, at Disney World, Loretta Ventro, who had taken her granddaughter on a long-awaited vacation, was watching on her phone, as the President began to pray. They had been waiting in a long line for almost an hour, and the child was playing with some other kids nearby but had gotten a little too far away. Loretta loudly said, "All right, Miss Kaylor! That's far enough. Get back over here."

As the child returned, she took her small hands in her own and began to kneel. Someone from behind asked what was going on, and she wordlessly showed them her phone, which showed the President in prayer. At that moment, phones started to make alert noises, and throughout the park, many went to their knees in prayer. The child, who never closed her eyes, looked around as most of the people in the park began to pray. She asked her grandmother, "MeeMaw, what's everyone doing?"

Her grandmother opened her eyes and took in the sight. She had never seen anything like it herself. She grabbed the child and held her close as she said, "This is us at our best." With pride, she closed her eyes and continued to pray.

⁂

In a small hospital, in a rural part of the country, Susie was sitting in a waiting room, while her husband, Buford, was having some blood work done. Some children, who were waiting with their parents, had taken notice of her. One of her gifts was her instant connection with children. They always seemed to love her. Before long, she was playing with all the children in the waiting room as their parents looked on. As she was watching them, a nurse entered with a remote in hand and changed the television channel. The nurse said, "Something's going on. I was told to turn it to a news channel."

When Susie read the screen and saw the President in prayer, she stopped and immediately turned and kneeled. Several of the children wanted to join her, even though they did not fully understand what was going on. As Susie prayed with the children, one mother came and angrily jerked her child away. The boy cried as the mother glared at Susie and said, "We don't believe in God, and I don't appreciate you corrupting my child with your beliefs."

Susie didn't respond. The child jerked his hand away from his mother and came back to the small group and kneeled again. The mother, exasperated, motioned to him with her hand, looked at Susie, and exclaimed, "Look what you've done!? What do you have to say for yourself?!"

Susie thought for a moment. Then, she replied calmly, "He said a child will lead them."

With that, Susie and the children continued to pray. Slowly, the other parents and nurses joined them. The angry mom refused to join, but she didn't stop her son from praying with Susie.

Across parks in major cities, at offices in large buildings, in factories in the Midwest and in shops in small towns everywhere, many joined their president. Without fully knowing or understanding it, they were all making a difference.

Chapter Thirty-Four

OUTSKIRTS OF JERUSALEM, ISRAEL

C ain smiled broadly. David was on his knees now, and the demons were pushing down hard on him. Cain wanted to say something more, but inside, he was touched by his master's power. He thought, I have said enough. I am ready for this man to finally die. With the blade raised high overhead, he swung downward with all his might. The blade stopped within an inch of David's forehead. Cain tried to pull it back, but now he was paralyzed and couldn't move. The demons overhead hissed and let out a shrill scream in unison.

From the tip of Cain's blade, a small light emerged. The light grew and spread across both Cain and David. As the light continued to grow, angels were suddenly visible, and they were everywhere. Both Cain and David could see light emerge out of the darkness in all directions. Both men were shocked at the sight of darkness turning to light all around them. The Heavenly host had arrived to protect David. They were holding Cain's blade in place, as the demons were holding David's.

As the light continued to spread, dozens of angels were visible, and they were forming a barrier around David. Illuminated, more demons were now becoming visible, and they began to fight with the angels. Between David and Cain, a power was growing, each was still frozen, but straining to break free. David's and Cain's eyes met, and both were filled with determination. All around, the sounds of fighting could be heard, but now they were just focused on each other. A wave of power was building between them that kept growing. Suddenly, both men were thrown in opposite directions as their blades spun away in the air.

When David came to his feet, he was alone in the dark. In the distance, high overhead, he could still see the angels and demons fighting with each other, but their battle was moving higher into the air and into the distance. David walked back in the general direction he had come from cautiously. He heard Cain's voice. It was calm and deliberate. "Here, in the darkness, is my home. You cannot win. We have been planning this for too long. Your god has forsaken you. Our demons are killing your angels as we speak, and now, you will die at my master's hand."

David could hear and feel something all around him. He instinctively hit and kicked in different directions, but he only hit air. A sinister laugh came out of the black void, and he heard Cain's voice again, "The end is near. Your time has come."

David felt his hands begin to shake. He knew he had to get control, had to focus. He drew in a deep breath of air. Then, he slowly fell to his knees and closed his eyes.

The laughter continued. Cain's voice boomed out of the darkness, "He can't help you now. It's just you and me. It's just me."

As David asked God for help, it was given to him. Something told him to reach forward, onto the ground. David moved his hands through the sand. Then, he felt his blade. He slowly pulled the handle into the palm of his right hand. He could feel Cain moving up behind him. He didn't know how, but he could sense it. He gripped the blade tightly, and with lightning speed, David jumped to his feet, turned, and swung. Cain was caught off guard but recovered as their blades met several times.

In the dark, the men were barely visible to one another, but both were parrying and countering with blinding speed. As this continued David was moving at a pace Cain could not match. Cain started being pushed back by David and felt himself giving ground. Now he was totally on the defensive and losing steam. Suddenly, David swung across Cain's body, and Cain's eyes went wide. David had sliced all the way across his torso. Cain immediately dropped his sword and looked at David with shock as his legs fell right and his upper body fell left. David, his chest heaving and his arms shaking, looked into Cain's wide eyes as he took his last breath and said, "Go to hell!"

Chapter Thirty-Five

PETRA, JORDAN

Eve could not explain it, but for some reason, she didn't feel fear. She had prayed and had felt God's presence. In the space of just a few seconds, she realized nothing could happen to her that he didn't allow. As the Chairman's blade came down toward her, Eve heard a gunshot. She heard the blade go to the ground, and she heard the Chairman scramble away. Then, Eve felt a hand on her shoulder, Ellen had finally caught up to her. She came to Eve's side and said, "Sorry. I fell. I think I broke my arm."

Eve tried to dry her eyes as she replied, "I don't know if they had an escape plan, but I don't think he will leave without her. I'm going after him. You take care of her." Eve forced herself to her feet and staggered off after Judas.

Ellen looked around and saw the Chairman's sword on the ground. Her left arm was broken, and she was cradling it with her right. She put her pistol back in its holster for a moment, picked up the sword, and swung it against the side of a nearby rock, breaking it. As she turned, she felt something hit her in the stomach. Without understanding what was happening, she felt herself fall to her knees.

The Chairman had picked up Eve's knife and had stabbed the soldier deep in her abdomen, coming in just under her bulletproof vest. The

Chairman reached down, pulled the gun from Ellen's holster, and threw it into the darkness. Furiously, she grabbed Ellen's head with both of her hands, pulled her up, and screamed into her face, "That sword has been in my family for centuries! Centuries! You think you are capable of killing me?! Killing me?! You are so far beneath me, my foot can't even step on you! You are nothing! Your god is nothing! Nothing!"

Ellen, her eyes closed, was praying hard and mumbling to herself.

The Chairman had lifted her up but had now let her fall back to her knees again. Outraged at being ignored, she said, "Pray all you want, but you are finished! You are dead!" She looked at Ellen in disgust and said, "You fool, what could you possibly be praying for now?!"

Ellen, still holding the handle of the broken sword in her right hand, exploded upward and, with an upper-cutting motion, drove the broken blade into the Chairman's abdomen with the last of her strength. The Chairman instinctively grabbed Ellen by the shoulders, and they fell back on their knees together. Ellen's left hand was on the Chairman's right shoulder, and her right hand, still on the hilt, was pushing upward with all her might. The two women, continuing their hold onto each other, slowly collapsed onto each other.

Ellen let her head fall onto the Chairman's shoulder. A shocked expression was fixed on the Chairman's face as Ellen whispered into her ear, "I was praying for strength, and God was listening."

The two women, holding each other, fell to the ground. As their lives ended, they each began a journey, in opposite directions, into eternity.

Eve was hurting all over. She had been cut twice. Her nose was broken and still bleeding. She blinked away tears as she pushed herself through the tunnel. Her rib and her legs ached, but she kept going. She remembered her promise to David, and she was going to push herself to the end. She couldn't run anymore, so she slowed to a walk. She gulped in air through her mouth, which hurt every time she had to breathe. She stopped, put her hand on the wall for balance. Then, she fell onto one knee. She tried to control her breathing. Her heart was racing.

With a groan, she pushed herself to her feet and kept walking. She could see a small light in the distance and realized this was another way out. She continued to walk until she moved through the opening. As she staggered through, she could feel sunlight on her face. She looked around and saw a helicopter in the distance. Her eyes met Judas's eyes. His disfigurement caused her to gasp. It was like looking at a real-life demon, only his eyes looked human. His head and face were so badly burned, even his nose looked like it was gone. Judas, while staring at her, said to the pilot, "The Chairman is dead. We need to leave now."

The pilot started the helicopter, and the blades began to slowly spin. Eve could hear the hum of the engine and see the blades slowly start to turn. She pulled out her back-up gun, her last weapon, and staggered as fast as her feet would go toward the helicopter. She was still over fifty yards away, and the helicopter blades were starting to spin faster. She was so exhausted. She stumbled and fell. She pushed herself up to her knees. She pulled the gun up to shoot, but her hands shook badly. She felt despair fill her, but she tried to shake it off. She sucked in another breath of air and, while in physical agony, prayed out loud, "Guide my hands, Lord!"

She pulled the trigger and didn't stop until every bullet was gone. She dropped the gun and just looked at the helicopter. The blades were spinning quickly, but it never took off. She watched in disbelief for a few more seconds. Then, she pushed herself to her feet and staggered toward it. She had no weapon, but she had come too far to stop now.

As she approached the helicopter, she could see what happened. Her bullets had killed the pilot. She staggered to the front of the helicopter, reached in, and shut off the motor. She felt her strength leaving her again. As she moved along the side of the helicopter, she saw Judas. He was holding the baby.

She was still breathing hard. She fell to her knees, and they just stared at each other for a moment. For a few awkward seconds, she thought she may have shot the baby, but then, he began to cry. Eve looked at Judas and wondered why he was not attacking her. Then, she saw the blood. One of her bullets had hit him in the chest. She had no strength to fight him or even to take the baby from him. After a few moments, in a shaky, hoarse voice, she asked, "What are you going to do?"

Judas, his calm unnerving her, said, "I will have to break his neck. I can't give him to you. He is destined to be with me. Where I go, he has to follow."

Eve felt a tear stream down her face. She didn't know what to say. She prayed for God to guide her, to give her the words. What came out of her mouth surprised them both. Eve said, "You loved David's mother? Didn't you?"

Eve wasn't sure where that came from, but Judas stroked the child's head and looked at him intently as he responded, "More than anything on Earth."

Eve's mind raced, and she said, "You know she would not want this child to die like this. She would not want the child to die by your hand."

He looked up at her and said, "I have already killed one son and tried to kill the other."

Eve said, "Maybe this is your chance to make up for it. Maybe this is your chance to do something on the way out to make it right."

He slowly shook his head and said, "No. I don't want to kill him, but I won't let him fall into the hands of the enemy."

Eve, still uncertain about what to say, replied, "His future is not certain. No matter what happens, no one knows what path he will choose. The choice will be his. Do you want to deprive him of that opportunity? If he is destined to serve your master, then why don't you give him the chance to decide that for himself?"

Judas just continued to stare at him, while cradling his head with his left hand.

Eve sensed she needed to continue, but desperation was filling her. "You could do both. By letting him live, you could do something to make right all the bad you have done, and in the end, he might choose your path anyway."

He looked up at her for a moment, as if considering her words.

Eve didn't know what else to say. As tears started to stream down her face, she said, "Please! Don't kill this defenseless child. Don't kill your grandson. Do one last thing for her. What you are holding in your arms is the legacy the two of you created."

The life was slowly ebbing out of him, which seemed to, somehow, soften him. Judas looked at her for a moment, feeling his hand around the child's neck. He gave the neck a soft squeeze. He still had the strength to break it, of that he was certain. He thought about his life and how it was ending. He seemed to have lost everything, failed at everything in the end. Now, as he made his final decision, he could choose life or death for his grandson. He closed his eyes, sucked in a deep breath of air. Then, he asked, "You will take him to his father?"

Eve wasn't sure what to say, so she just nodded.

Judas slowly nodded and replied, "Very well then."

Shock washed over Eve as she grabbed the side of the helicopter for leverage and grunted to come to her feet. She reached in slowly and put her arms around the baby. For a moment, Judas seemed to resist, and as he and Eve exchanged a look, she said, "It's okay. I've got him."

Judas slowly released his grasp, and she pulled him away. When she was sure she had him, she let out a gasp and staggered backward, falling onto her knees again. Judas's head fell back against the wall behind him, and he looked over at her. She looked down at the child and began to weep.

After a few moments, she looked up and saw Judas was staring at them both. She wasn't sure what to say, so she asked, "Can I pray with you?"

Judas slowly shook his head and said, "No, it's too late for me."

She stared for a moment. Then, she said, "It's never too late."

Ignoring her reply, Judas said, "Tell David that I did it for his mother."

With that, his head fell forward. As his chin rested against his chest, Eve knew he was gone.

Chapter Thirty-Six

ШASHIПG†OП, D.C.

The President was preparing for a press conference in the Rose Garden. He was talking to Calebs. "Try to let the blame fall squarely on me. I don't want anyone else going down for this."

Calebs nodded and said, "Of course, sir."

After the two men exchanged a warm look, the President gave his vice-president a firm handshake and said, "Get ready."

With that, he walked to the podium and began, "My fellow Americans, the last few hours have seen extraordinary military and political action. I am glad to say, we have stopped a major war from happening. With our forces entering the Middle East, a great battle has been prevented. We have been informed, as of an hour ago, a cease fire is now in place. We plan to enter into negotiations with the Arab people, and with the cooperation we have been promised from both China and Russia, we believe we can broker a peace deal and end this conflict. However, there is still much to do. I have dispatched the secretary of state to the Middle East to begin the process." He looked around and drew in a long breath. "As you know, we took unprecedented action this morning. We are still sifting through the information, but it looks as if we are finding the greatest conspiracy, the greatest internal threat our nation has ever faced, has been eradicated.

"On my orders, every one of these prisoners is being held in a maximum-security prison at an undisclosed location. I have already begun speaking with the various governors about replacing or having new elections for the many members of Congress that have been indicted."

He took another long breath and said, "As I stated this morning, everything done was legal, but I know there will be those that will say it was not. I have enjoyed being your president these last four years. I have learned a lot about leadership in that time. Leadership is tough. It takes courage, and I have recently learned, true leadership takes faith. Because we need our focus to be on these traitors and the vast conspiracy we are uncovering, I feel I must now practice the loneliest form of leadership — sacrifice. You know, one of the best things I did when I ran for reelection was keep a great vice-president. This evening, at five, I will tender my resignation, and I will step aside and leave you in the very capable hands of our vice-president, Jerry Calebs."

With this, Calebs approached the podium, walking with his stiff leg and using his cane. He and the President shared a brief handshake, then a hug, and Calebs moved to the microphone. As he began his prepared remarks, the President moved away and down a long hallway. He stopped for a moment and looked back, realizing he had these moments to himself.

On one end was the press conference, and on the other, his Secret Service detail waited for him. But, here, he was alone. He stopped and thought about everything for a moment. He thought he would be sad, but for some reason, he wasn't. He thought of the last twenty-four hours and realized the scope of what he had accomplished. Then, he thought about his personal life and how, in the midst of all this, he had found himself and his purpose again. He realized the supreme irony his life had become. He was a man who had lost it all and yet found everything. He began to walk again, knowing he still had many years ahead of him, and now, he also had found purpose. As he walked down the long hallway, all alone, he pumped a fist into the air and said, "Praise God!" He looked up and said, "Your will is done, Lord!"

EPILOGUE

⁓

David came walking out of the dunes and back to the battle, but it was over now. As he heard jets scream overhead, he saw a large number of men and women on their knees, with hands on the back of their heads. David saw Job, who had taken charge. Job approached David, gave him a firm handshake, and asked, "Cain?"

David replied, "He's dead." Job nodded as David asked, "Where's the Apostle?"

Job replied, "He didn't make it."

David knew it was possible, but he didn't want to believe it. He thought for a moment. After reflecting, he said, "He never gave up on us, did he?"

Surprising David, Job said, "Neither did you."

A large helicopter slowly flew in and landed in the distance, and several soldiers got out. Job motioned for them, and they came in his direction. When the first soldier reached him, Job asked, "Where is the Chairman?"

The soldier replied, "Dead. They fought to the last. We left none alive."

David was staring toward the helicopter now when he saw Eve get off carrying his baby. David broke into a run. Eve smiled broadly as David reached her. Giving him his child, she said, "Meet your son."

David, beaming, took him and was instantly overcome with emotion. As he looked into the face of the infant, he thought of Ruth and her sacrifice. Then, he felt tears. He stroked the baby's head and could not seem to stop smiling. Holding the child tightly in his right arm, he reached his left arm around Eve, giving her a firm hug, and said, "Thank you."

Eve nodded, wiped away tears and smiled broadly. David turned, took in the battlefield, then holding his son closely, looked at the setting sun. In that moment, God told him what he had to do. The great battle had ended, and the Satanists, at least for now, were defeated. This child would be his life. He owed that to God. He owed that to her. She had given her life for him to live and now in a sense, so would David. Job was at his side now, and he said, "David, I would like you to join us. Make it official. I think you and I both know that is what God wants."

David turned and said, "I think your mission is over. The Satanists have been defeated. There is nothing left of them."

Job said, "As long as Lucifer lives, there will always be more Satanists. He will have to start over now, but he will be back, and we will remain ready to protect the faithful."

David looked at his child and said, "No. Thank you but no. I have to be a father now. This child's future is my responsibility."

Job, surprised, said, "David, you can't just walk away. You can't just leave. After all that has happened, how could you even consider it?"

David replied, "I want to raise my child. I want to take care of him. I have to be a mom and a dad to him."

Job said, "You know there is still a chance he could be the Anti-Christ."

David paused for a moment, but then, he ignored this and turned to walk away.

Job asked, "What will you do with him? Where will you go?"

David turned and said, "I'm going to cover him, cover him in the blood of Jesus." David turned and began to walk away again.

Job screamed, "Do you really think you can walk away from us?! From everything?! Do you really think you can just live a normal life now?!"

David turned for the last time and replied, "Just watch me."

He turned and walked away, carrying his child and beginning the last battle of his life, the battle for his son's soul. Now, he had the clarity that had eluded him for most of his life. This child would have free will, which meant in the end, he would still choose his own path. But that was a long time in the future. David would make sure he knew God and understood his teachings.

As Job, Eve, and several others looked on, David and his son walked away, into the setting sun. Eve watched as he moved further into the distance. When she spoke, she felt she was speaking for more than herself. She was speaking for David's mother, for David's brother, and she knew she was speaking for Ruth, when she muttered, to no one in particular, "Well done, David. Well done."

✝HE END

CPSIA information can be obtained
at www.ICGtesting.com
Printed in the USA
JSHW021415170622
27188JS00002B/78

9 781039 116887